FOOL'S PLAY

Royce rides into Jawbone looking for a doctor, but finds trouble. Living by the gun can he expect anything else? He signs on with land baron Yale Jamerson, hoping for a job that will leave his conscience clear. However, when Jamerson plans to dam the river and charge road tolls, the townspeople revolt. Forced to choose between his livelihood and his conscience, Royce must decide which path to take. Will it lead to a showdown with his closest friend?

CARL WILLIAMS

FOOL'S PLAY

Complete and Unabridged

LINFORD
Leicester

First published in Great Britain in 2010 by
Robert Hale Limited
London

First Linford Edition
published 2012
by arrangement with
Robert Hale Limited
London

British Library CIP Data

Williams, Carl.
  Fool's play.- -(Linford western library)
  1. Western stories.
  2. Large type books.
  I. Title II. Series
  823.9′2–dc23

ISBN 978–1–4448–1025–7

Published by
F. A. Thorpe (Publishing)
Anstey, Leicestershire

Set by Words & Graphics Ltd.
Anstey, Leicestershire
Printed and bound in Great Britain by
T. J. International Ltd., Padstow, Cornwall

This book is printed on acid-free paper

1

Royce was hurting; he'd been riding all day, which was now nearly spent. His left hand reached behind him to hold his back a minute, and his fingers felt the pellet beneath the skin. He sorely wanted to get it out, and he aimed to, soon as he got to Jawbone.

His horse plodded on through the knee-high grass. The countryside had a slight roll to it, just enough to vary the rhythm of a long ride. In the far distance he made out the jagged, hazy top of a mountain range. No sign anywhere of any kind of civilization, not until he spotted the scrawny, crooked posts standing in a row across the prairie.

When Royce finally got within a few feet of the barbed wire, his horse stopped without having to be reined in. He looked both ways down the fence line, south and north: no gate in sight. Then he checked behind him and scanned the land ahead: absolutely no one anywhere. Good. He didn't want to get shot for what he was about to do.

Slowly dismounting, being careful of his back, Royce opened his saddle-bag and took out a pair of wire cutters. He quickly cut the three strands of wire at a point right next to the post. After leading his horse across the downed wires, he turned and pulled each wire back to the post, stretching it a little tighter than before so he could hammer the barbs into the wood with the flat of his cutters.

Another few miles and he came to a river, though it was hardly a river any more. The riverbed looked to be eighty feet across, but the water was running about twelve feet wide in the deepest part of the channel.

Funny, thought Royce. Here in early summer the water should be flowing higher than this from the snowmelt in those distant mountains. Fording the stream was no problem. He didn't even get his stirrups wet.

He started seeing cattle now, scattered in lazy clusters across the land, with some coming down toward the river to drink. He checked the brand on the flank of one of the passing cows. YJ — that would be right. He'd heard the big spread in these parts belonged to Yale Jamerson.

Royce followed the river as it curved northwest, knowing it would lead him to Jawbone. There was about an hour's worth of daylight left, and he was hoping to reach town before full dark. He didn't care to spend another night on the hard ground, not with that pellet moving around, sticking him now and again.

The very last tinge of reddish gold was fading when Royce rode into Jawbone. Lights glowed in many of the town's windows. Coming down from a low rise in the deepening dusk, he saw two main streets and five or six narrow cross streets or alleys separating a

3

number of houses and various two-story structures of unknown usage, no doubt including a couple of saloons, and maybe a bank and a barber shop. He hoped most of all for a hotel and a café, since he hadn't slept or eaten much in days, and he had no more taste for jerky.

The livery stable wasn't hard to find. A young fella, fifteen or sixteen and looking bored, hopped up when Royce rode in and eased off his horse.

'I don't know who looks more tuckered out, mister . . . you or your horse.'

'Yeah, well, we took turns riding each other.'

The young man laughed, probably more because he wanted to than because of the joke itself. Royce allowed a smile.

'You can put him up, I suppose. Feed him, groom him.'

'That's what we do, Pa and me. Take care of horses. How's his shoes?' He bent over to look.

'His shoes are fine,' said Royce. 'Better'n mine.' He got another easy laugh. 'What's your name?'

'Axel. And no, not like a wagon axle,' he said quickly. 'My Pa came from Sweden, and Axel's a regular name over there.'

Royce nodded. 'Nothing wrong with a name like that. So tell me, Axel, where can a man get a good meal in this town?'

'The only place to get a *good* meal is Betsy's Café, but she closes at sundown.'

Royce glanced behind him. The sky was full dark now.

'Betsy have to get home to her mother?'

Axel gave another laugh. 'Betsy's a hundred years old. Naw, more like sixty. But she don't stay up late. Gets up early, though, and opens for breakfast.'

'Any place else to get fed?'

'Just one, a saloon.'

'I'd rather stay out of saloons.'

''Cause you don't drink?'

''Cause other men do. But if it's the only place . . . '

'It's The Last Apache, right down the street on the left.'

'Last Apache, huh?' Royce figured there was a story behind that name, but he was too hungry and too worn out to ask.

'They serve a tol'able stew.'

'Then that's where I'll go.' He unhitched his saddle-bags and pulled his Winchester from its boot.

'Pa says carrying guns is dangerous.'

'More dangerous not to.' He handed the reins to Axel. 'He's all yours 'til tomorrow.' Then he turned to leave.

'Oh, mister, Pa says everybody's got to pay in advance. Just in case.'

'In case of what?'

'I don't know. In case of anything.'

'Your Pa's a smart man. How much?'

'For feed and grooming and a stall, one dollar.'

'Kinda high.'

'It's good feed . . . honest. And I'll take good care of him.'

'I believe you will, Axel.'

Royce fished a dollar coin from his pocket and tossed it to the boy, then walked out into the street, still wishing he didn't have to go to the saloon to eat. He'd seen too many bad things happen in saloons during the sixteen years he'd been wandering the West.

As he approached The Last Apache, he saw it was well lit inside. That eased his mind a little. Still, his right hand moved out of habit to touch the handle of his Colt where it rested in a holster and gunbelt that hadn't been more than an arm's length away in many years.

He stepped through the door and stopped just inside, quickly taking everything in. The bar was on the right, fairly long but nothing fancy: one man standing behind the bar, a cowboy and a younger man standing near the far end; the bottom steps of a staircase just beyond the bar; four tables in a row along the left side; two men at the first one, four at the second, two at the third, and nobody at the last one. About half the men wore guns. No piano in the room — that was good. And no women lounging around — that was even better. They had a way of stirring things up.

As Royce headed for the empty table, glad that it was at the back, he felt the eyes of the other men on him, sizing him up. All of his six-foot frame covered in trail dust, a four day growth of beard on his face, saddle-bags over his left shoulder, Winchester in his left hand, right hand hanging free and ready — he knew how he looked to them but nobody said anything to him.

When he got to the last table, Royce dropped his saddlebags, stood his Winchester in the corner, and sat down with his back to the wall, facing the bar. Every bit of bone and flesh suddenly gave in to fatigue. He slowly took off his low-crowned hat, laid it on the table, then ran a weary hand through his hair.

'Get something for you?' called the bartender with the blunt friendliness of a merchant.

'I hear you've got stew.'

'That we do, and I eat it myself.'

'I'll have some of what you haven't eaten. And a beer.'

Now that everybody had looked him over, they must've decided he wasn't worth any more attention, because they went back to their conversations. The big cowboy at the bar was wrangling with the younger man.

'I'm telling you, Dan, that's the way I did it.'

'Well, I don't believe it.'

'No more'n three years back.'

'Seems like somebody would've heard about it.'

'Plenty of folks did, but that was over two hundred miles from here.'

Royce tried to ignore them and was glad when the bartender brought his food. The beer was slightly cool, probably from being stored in a root cellar. The meat-heavy stew came in a wide bowl, and he savored the first several bites.

'You're sayin' I'm a liar.'

'No, I never said that.'

'If you don't believe what a man says, you're calling him a liar.'

As the voices at the bar grew louder, the other conversations in the room stopped. Royce saw the younger man was only about nineteen years old. He was of medium height, but skinny in comparison with the other man's bulk. Even so, he wasn't backing down.

'Maybe you believe what you're saying, but I don't. That's the difference.'

'I'm telling you I faced him down, and he had the biggest reputation of any man in that county. The whole state.'

'Sure, Blake. If you say so.'

The one called Blake took on a more sinister tone. 'I think maybe I'll run you out of town the same way, just to show you.'

'I'm not wearing a gun, so it wouldn't be the same.'

'He wasn't wearing his, either. He had laid it down on the bar, showing it off. Just a minute.' Blake stepped quickly to the table where the four men sat. 'Loan me your six-gun, Sammy.'

Sammy looked around at a well dressed man in his fifties who gave him a little nod. Sammy handed over the gun.

Blake went back to face Dan and set the gun on the bar.

'That's how he had it. And now I'll say to you what I said to him. Pick it up.

The young man glanced over at the gun. 'I don't want to.'

'Then you're a coward.'

'I'm not a coward.'

'I say you are.'

He gave Dan a tremendous shove, sending him sprawling along the bar and down to the floor on one knee. Furious, Dan scrambled to his feet, stepping up even with the gun.

'Go ahead,' said Blake.

Dan's hand edged on to the bar, hesitating, but moving closer to the gun.

Royce stopped chewing and sat in wonderment. He couldn't believe somebody was really pulling this old trick. And yet he'd seen foolish men goaded into it before. This kid was gonna get killed for sure.

Blake had set himself in a stance with his hand by his holster. Royce could almost see young Dan silently talking himself into believing he could get to the gun in time. And suddenly Royce just couldn't stand it.

'Don't do it, kid,' he said quietly.

Everyone's eyes shifted to Royce. Blake tilted his head as if unsure of what he'd heard.

'You say something, mister?'

Royce spoke to Dan. 'It's a fool's play. Nobody can pick up a gun off a flat surface faster than a man can draw from a holster. If this fella says he backed somebody down that way, then he probably did, if the other fella had any sense.'

Blake turned toward Royce now. 'Are you looking for trouble?'

'No, I brought it with me.'

Royce was sorry the instant he said it, because he could tell from Blake's face he took it as a challenge, when really it was just a weary observation to himself that trouble seemed to ride along wherever he went, like a saddle companion with no other place to go.

'I see you're wearing a holster. Why don't you stand up and draw if you think I'm nothing special?'

'I don't know if you're special or not. And I don't care. Right now I just want to eat my stew.'

'You know what? I'm gonna shoot somebody. It can either be this kid, or it can be you. What do you say to that?'

Royce wasn't sure he even had the strength to stand up. But more than being worn out by all the miles, he was worn out from seeing men like Blake push other men around. With an effort he slowly rose to his feet. He figured if he beat him, he could get back to his stew. And if not, at least he wouldn't have to suffer exhaustion any more, or pain, or hunger and thirst.

He waited, stone still, watching for the telltale twitch in the other man's shoulder, because the shoulder nearly always came up a bit just as the gun hand went into motion. With Blake it wasn't hard to see. The big shoulder suddenly hunched. Automatically, in a practiced reflex with no thought whatsoever, Royce's hand swept his Colt out of its holster and instantly blasted a slug into his opponent's chest, slamming him back against the bar. Blake's gun fired wide, splintering the top slat of a chair at Royce's table. Then Blake slumped straight down, his back against the bar, until he landed sitting upright on the floor, dead.

Royce scanned the faces of the other men. No one was moving. Dan gaped at him as if he'd never seen such a thing — he probably hadn't. The older man at the second table fixed him with an appraising look, and a man sitting at his elbow was actually grinning. Royce didn't like the look of that one. He wore polished black boots and a pearl-studded shirt, and his holster looked sleek, designed for speed.

'I guess now I'll have to take on all his friends,' muttered Royce.

The older man laughed. 'No need to worry about that. He didn't have any.'

With those words the other men in the room relaxed from the moment's tension. Nothing more was going to happen. Royce holstered his gun and sat back down to his stew. The cowboy who loaned his gun to Blake retrieved it from the bar, and the older man motioned to him.

'Sammy, take Blake down to the undertaker. You help him, George.'

The fourth man from the table rose, leaving just the older man and the fancied-up cowboy, if that's what he was. Sammy and George carried Blake out of the saloon. The two men at the table next to Royce's got up and left. Royce kept eating his stew. The older man rose and walked over.

'I've got to admire a man who can

kill somebody and go right back to eating his supper. That tells me something.'

'It tells you I'm mighty hungry.'

'You got a name? One you'd like to share?'

'Royce. And I'm guessing your name's Jamerson.'

'That's pretty good guessing,' he said, pushing aside the chair Blake shot and pulling up another to sit down. 'How'd you figure it?'

'The way your man Sammy looked to you for an OK before he loaned Blake his gun. You're known for owning things around here.'

'Not everything.'

'Blake would've killed young Dan for sure.'

'Most likely.'

'That didn't bother you?'

'I don't make other men's decisions for them.'

'You gave the nod.'

'But Dan didn't have to go for the gun. And he might not have.'

'Some choice for a young man to make. Be humiliated or be dead.'

Dan had followed Sammy and George to the door of the saloon, watching as they carried out Blake's body. After hesitating, he came over to Royce's table, stopping a few feet away, glancing more warily at Jamerson than at Royce.

'I reckon I should thank you.'

'No need, but accepted. Just one thing, young Dan. If you expect to be old Dan someday, don't argue with men wearing guns in saloons.'

Dan nodded and backed away, then turned and left the saloon.

Jamerson watched as Royce finished up his stew. 'Where you headed?'

'To bed, if I can find one.'

'I thought you might be looking for a job. It so happens, as of a couple minutes ago, I have an opening.'

'What did Blake do for you? Besides entertain you.'

'What he did doesn't have to be what you do.'

'What you want me to do, most likely, is the sort of thing *he* does,' said Royce, nodding toward the fancy cowboy.

'Malone?'

At the mention of his name, Malone raised a forefinger to the brim of his hat in mock salute, accompanied by a smirky smile.

'What Malone does, you don't need to concern yourself with.'

'I hope that's right.' Royce glanced at Malone once more. 'He sure smiles a lot.'

Jamerson said, ''One may smile, and smile, and be a villain.' That's from Shakespeare's *Hamlet*.'

'Is your man Malone a villain?'

'Everything's open to interpretation. In *Julius Caesar* Shakespeare wrote about a man who had 'a lean and hungry look' and said 'such men are dangerous'. Would you like another bowl of stew?'

'No, thanks. All I'd like right now is to get a night's sleep on something more comfortable than sagebrush.'

'I keep a room here, upstairs, for when I stay over in town. I'm riding back to my ranch tonight. You can have the room. No obligation.'

Royce took a few seconds to mull it over, longing for that bed.

'The door locks,' said Jamerson. 'The key's inside.'

'OK,' he said. 'Thanks.'

'Room 4 at the far end of the hall.' Jamerson stood up. 'Come to the ranch tomorrow. Ask anyone how to get there.'

Royce nodded once. Then Jamerson signaled to Malone, and they both headed out. Just before he followed Jamerson through the door, Malone looked back and smiled.

Royce climbed the stairs slowly and trudged along the narrow hall to room 4, just alongside a back stairway that lcd down to the alley. He cautiously opened the door. Dim light filtered in through the window, but otherwise the room was dark. He searched in his pocket for matches and lit the coal-oil lamp on the bureau, revealing a key lying beside it. He turned the key in the door lock and left it there. Then he hung his gunbelt on the headboard post, pulled off his boots and collapsed on to the bed, immediately falling into a deep sleep.

An hour later a knock sounded on the door. It was a soft knock, and it didn't penetrate his exhausted mind. Then the knock came louder, and Royce roused. One more time and he was on his feet, gun in hand, moving toward the door. There was light in the room, and he realized he had left the lamp burning. He turned the key, then jerked open the door about six inches.

A woman drew back with a gasp. 'Where's Yale?'

'Jamerson?'

'You're in his room.'

Royce understood now and lowered his revolver. 'He's at his ranch. Said I could use the room.' He opened the door a little wider.

The woman, very attractive in her mid-twenties, pulled her shawl a little tighter across her chest as he looked at her.

'I don't come with the room,' she said.

'No offense, but I'm too tired to care.'

She studied him a moment with a wordless frown, then turned aside and headed down the back staircase, moving quietly. Royce locked the door again and blew out the lamp. Once more he fell on to the bed, plunging into a dark current that quickly swept him away.

2

Royce woke up looking into a gun barrel. He jerked his head back sharply, then realized it was his own gun lying on the pillow beside him. He had neglected to holster it the night before when he was too tired to think straight. He sat up in bed and shook himself as the memories returned. Had he really killed someone last night? And the woman at the door . . . had that been just a dream?

A sudden pain stabbed him on the left side of his back, reminding him of what had brought him to Jawbone. He'd heard there was a doctor here.

There was a wash basin in the room, so he cleaned himself up and shaved his whiskers, leaving only his mustache. Hungry again, he recalled Axel telling him about Betsy's Café being open for breakfast. He picked up his gear, left the key on the bureau, and went down the back staircase to the alley.

At Betsy's he had strong black coffee, eggs and ham, biscuits and gravy. Axel had been right about the grub — it was good. And Betsy did look on the downhill side of sixty.

When she refilled his cup of coffee, she said, 'Are you the fella who saved Danny Winston from getting himself gunned down last night?'

'I guess maybe I am.'

'That's a good thing you did.'

'Killing a man's hardly ever a good thing.'

'Better it was that no-good cowboy than Danny. You shot one, but you saved one. That evens out the score, I'd say.'

'I've never been much on keeping score.' He asked her then about the doctor.

'That would be Doc Haney. Has a house on the west side of town, at the far end of the next street over.'

'Why so far out?'

'So folks won't hear all the screams from his patients.' She watched for his reaction and seemed disappointed she didn't get one. 'He's a good doctor, as long as you don't have too much wrong with you. And you don't look all that sick.'

'If I had been, these biscuits would've fixed me up. Been a long time since I had biscuits good as these.'

'I love bein' sweet-talked. Too bad it's always over my cookin'.' She shook her head and moved away to her other customers.

Royce found the doctor's house as soon as he finished breakfast. The placard nailed next to the front door said: DOCTOR REUBEN HANEY, GENERAL MEDICINE. Haney, a man of late middle age, came to the door himself.

'Most folks are too lazy to get sick this early in the day,' he said, leading Royce into his examining room.

'Not sick. Just gunshot.'

The doctor glanced back around at

him with a quick look up and down.

'I don't see any holes. I thought Blake missed you.'

'So you heard about that.'

'Gunfights get talked about faster than anything, especially when it's one of Jamerson's men who got shot and the man who shot him didn't get shot himself.'

Royce took off his shirt. 'I've been shot, all right. Just not lately.' He turned and pointed to the spot in his back.

'You've got some scars back there, sure enough. Lie down on the table on your belly. Let me take a look at that.' He felt the bump under the skin. 'Must be old, 'cause there's no entry wound I can see. And it's not a bullet.'

'Buckshot,' said Royce. 'From a long time back. Got some of it out soon after it happened. A couple pellets deeper in worked their way to the surface later on. Now this one. I'd like to get it out.'

'I can do that.' He reached for some instruments and chuckled. 'Buckshot, you say. Come from stealing chickens or women?' When he didn't get an answer, he went on. 'I'd go for the chickens myself. At least they lay eggs. But I guess it's all a matter of taste. And age.'

Royce saw him open a bottle of chloroform. 'None of that.'

'I'm gonna do some cutting, you know.'

'I know.' Royce didn't want to be drugged and unsteady. He didn't like pain, but at least it quickened the senses.

'Men I cut on during the War would've given anything for chloroform.'

Royce didn't ask him which side of the War he'd done his cutting on. The soft Georgia accent, along with the fact he'd gone without a supply of chloroform, told him which side was more likely. Not that it mattered now. And besides, doctors weren't in the service of war. Royce had even been told a Yankee doctor tried to save his father, but lost him on the operating table in a field hospital.

'Here,' said Doc Haney, 'bite on this.'

He handed Royce a strip of rawhide. Royce saw it had more than one set of teeth prints in it.

'No, thanks.' Instead, he reached in his rear pocket and pulled out a bandanna, which he clamped between his teeth. It was none too clean, but at least the grime was his own.

The doctor rubbed the spot on Royce's back with a cool swab of alcohol. A second later he said, 'Here we go,' and his scalpel pierced the skin.

Royce grimaced, but the pain was bearable. It took less than a minute for Doc Haney to get hold of the pellet with his forceps and pull it out. Royce was just about to feel relieved when the doctor poured some alcohol on the incision. This time he grunted strongly.

'Just cleaning it out. This'll take a few stitches, so hang on.'

The sewing hurt worse than the cutting; Royce was sweating by the time it was done. Then Doc Haney had him sit up while he wrapped a bandage around him, tying it off with practiced fingers.

'There. That should do the job. Got any more of those in you?'

'Not that I know of. And if I do, they can just stay where they are, unless they start pinching me the way this one did.' He stood up and gingerly put on his shirt. 'How much?'

'Normally I'd charge three dollars, but I'll give you a dollar discount for shooting one of Jamerson's men. Too bad you didn't just wing him, though. I'd have had more business.'

'No, 'cause then he'd be in here and I'd be where he is.'

The doctor laughed. 'That's right enough.'

Royce paid the two dollars, which seemed like a bargain. Before he left, he thought about asking Doc Haney more about Jamerson, but didn't bother. He'd known men like Jamerson before, and had worked for them. And he figured he might again, depending on what he was asked to do.

Royce went to retrieve his horse from the livery stable and was greeted by a skinny Swede, who grinned at him as if he were a long-time friend.

'Some fight last night,' he said. 'I'm Ludie Lundstrom, Axel's father.'

'Pleased to meet you.'

'No, pleased to meet *you*. That Blake, he was no good. Nobody will miss that one.'

Royce didn't comment. Last night still seemed unreal to him. He'd been so groggy from the trail, it was as if he had watched somebody else do those things and not himself.

Lundstrom saddled his horse for him and led him out.

'Hope you're not leaving town already.'

'Not sure yet. Can you tell me how to get to Jamerson's ranch?'

The friendly smile of the Swede shrank away. 'What do you want to go out there for?'

'A job, maybe.'

Lundstrom looked disgusted. 'There's

a road north of town. Follow it and you'll come to Jamerson's place. Maybe he won't make you pay the toll.'

'Toll?'

'The road goes through his ranch and out the other side, toward the mountains. Anybody who travels that way has to pay a toll.'

'Doesn't seem right.'

'He's got enough guns to make it right.'

Royce nodded and spurred his horse north. The road pretty much followed the shallow river, sometimes close, sometimes farther away. The ranch was an hour's ride from town, or at least the toll gate was. He saw it up ahead, with fences stretching off to both sides. The fence on the right led down to the river, about a quarter mile away. There was a little shack next to the gate, and the gate was closed. As he approached, two men armed with rifles came out of the shack. Royce pulled up and waited to hear what they would say.

'Toll for a rider is four bits,' said one,

getting right down to business.

'Is there another road to the north?' asked Royce.

The other man laughed. 'If there was, we wouldn't make much money charging tolls, now would we? If you go north, you pay here.'

'Even if I've been invited?'

'Invited? By who?'

'Mr Jamerson.'

The men were skeptical. 'What for?'

'Blake's dead. I'm not.'

The men exchanged looks, then looked at Royce again with a new regard.

'Blake was good with a gun.'

Royce shrugged. 'He shot the hell out of a chair.'

'Well,' said one, 'if Mr Jamerson invited you.' He nodded to his friend, who swung open the gate.

'Thanks,' said Royce, riding on through and not looking back.

Another twenty minutes brought him to a side road that cut away to the west, where he saw a large house and barn and stock pens half a mile distant. Nobody challenged him as he rode up to the house, dismounted, and tied his horse to the rail. Apparently Jamerson felt secure here.

Royce stepped to the porch and knocked on the front door. A few seconds passed, then the door opened to reveal a woman in her middle years, still attractive, but clearly a beauty when she was younger. Royce took off his hat.

'Hello, ma'am. Is Mr Jamerson home?'

'Yes, he is. Why do you want to see him?'

'He said there might be a job for me here.'

She paused, looking at him intently. 'I see. Well . . . come in.' She stepped back, allowing him to enter, then took him into a medium sized room to one side of the entry hall. 'Wait here, Mr — ?'

'Royce.'

'You may have a seat until he comes.'

'Thank you, ma'am.'

She left him then, and he lowered himself into a big leather chair. There was a desk in the room, and shelves of books covered the walls. He had never seen so many books. He leaned sideways and was trying to read some of the titles when footsteps sounded behind him and Yale Jamerson walked in.

'Find anything there you like?'

Royce stood up. 'It's been a long time since I read a book.'

'You have that in common with a great many others in this part of the country. I've found books to be a great consolation. I have the classics, of course, but the modern writers, too.' He pulled a volume from a shelf. 'Mark Twain, for instance. Ever hear of him?'

'Heard the name.'

'This is *The Adventures of Tom Sawyer*. I especially enjoyed this one. In the evenings it took me away from all the hard things I had to do each day. It took me back to my own boyhood, when the things I faced were little more than trifling adventures.'

Jamerson regarded the book a moment longer, then returned it to its spot on the shelf. Motioning Royce to sit back down, he took a seat behind his desk.

'Literary tastes aside, I take it you've decided to accept my offer of employment.'

'I'm not sure. You didn't say what the job was, exactly.'

'You passed the toll gate, didn't you?'

'And used your name to keep my four bits.'

'There's another gate on the north side of my land. Besides ranching, I turn a nice sum from regulating the flow of commerce in this area.'

'Nobody rides through without paying, is that it?'

'Or carries freight, or drives herds, or transports goods of any kind. Every wagon, every rider — every man on foot, for that matter — pays for the privilege of crossing my land. There are some, of course, who object to this.

That's why I need men at the toll gates. Plus . . . '

'Plus what?'

'Believe it or not, we have a certain number of outlaws in these parts who attack my toll gates for the money. There are always some types of men who are willing to kill for the coins in a cashbox.'

'Or kill to protect those coins.'

Jamerson smiled. 'You have a wit about you. I appreciate that in a man, as well as skill with a gun.'

'So my gun and my wit would be guarding your toll money.'

'In the ordinary course of collecting the tolls, which naturally includes persuading any reluctant travelers to pay or turn back. And there may be other duties that arise from time to time.'

'Such as?'

'Riding fences. Some people try to avoid the toll by cutting my fences. I can't abide a fence cutter.' He leaned forward in his chair. 'By the way, how did you get to Jawbone?'

'I rode in.'

'From which direction?'

'East.'

'I've got all that land fenced.' He fixed Royce with a steady gaze.

'My horse is a good jumper.'

Jamerson smiled then. 'Yes, a definite wit.' He stood up. 'Pay is a dollar a day. You can stay in the bunkhouse or find a place of your own. No charge for the bunkhouse because I prefer having my men close by.'

'Bunkhouse will be fine,' said Royce, also standing. 'And obliged for the room last night.'

'A small investment that apparently paid off.'

Royce started to mention the woman who knocked on his door, but thought better of it. And the next moment he was glad.

'You met Sarah, of course.'

Royce looked at him blankly, not willing to commit himself.

'Mrs. Jamerson. She let you in.'

'I didn't know you were married.'

'Thirty-one years. Nothing takes the place of a good wife, Royce.'

But apparently some things could fill in for a night.

Royce went to settle in at the bunkhouse, where he picked out one of the unclaimed bunks. As he dropped his gear on the thin, straw-packed mattress, he heard a faint sound and turned to find Malone standing there.

'I see you're one of us now,' said Malone, smiling that small, funny-to-himself smile of his.

'I guess you could say that.'

Malone walked forward and held out his hand. 'Malone.'

Royce took his hand and they shook. 'Royce.'

'You were pretty fast last night when you went up against Blake.'

'I don't remember much about it.'

'Neither does Blake.'

'I didn't want to kill him,' said Royce.

'But you didn't mind it, either. Yale figured you'd hire on.'

'You call him Yale?'

'Mr Jamerson to his face. But Yale's shorter. Know how he got that name? His daddy went to Yale. The college back east.'

Royce nodded. 'Jamerson go there, too?'

'Only for a year, before he came out west to make his fortune.'

'By taxing other people out of theirs.'

'That came later, after thirty years of putting this spread together and after the town got built up.'

'You seem to know a lot about it.'

'Been with Yale over two years now. You can learn a lot in two years.'

Royce had never stayed anywhere in his adult life for two years, or even one. And the things he learned in the short time he stayed someplace were mostly things he'd rather not have known.

'You on guard duty, too?' asked Royce.

'From time to time. Gets kind of boring. Mostly I'm what you'd call Yale's troubleshooter. Whatever's troubling him, I shoot.' He laughed.

'Stay busy, do you?'

'Not so much any more.' He sounded disappointed. 'Anyway, welcome to the YJ. I'll introduce you to all the boys tonight.'

'Thanks.'

Malone started walking away, then stopped and turned. 'By the way, just so you'll know, Blake wasn't the fastest gun around here.'

'Lucky for me, since I was moving kinda slow last night.'

Malone grinned with a soundless chuckle and went on out.

3

Royce was put to work soon enough. At midday he and a cowboy named Charlie Ray rode to the toll gate on the north side of the YJ ranch and took over from two other men who'd been there since daybreak. Just like on the south side, there was a strong gate, a sturdy fence, and a shack for shelter. But up here there were a few scattered trees, and Royce saw even more as the land slowly rose in elevation farther north. He also noticed a wide sheen of water in the east, much broader than the river had been.

'What's that over there? The river?'

'Yes and no,' said Charlie Ray, a man of about forty who looked like he'd been through many hard times. 'The river's above it, and the river's below it. But right there it's all bunched up in a lake because of the dam.'

'A dam? Out here?'

'Nobody told you? Jamerson dammed the river a couple years back. A big, fancy dam, too. Strong as anything. Hired a man all the way from Kansas City to come figure it out.'

'Why did Jamerson want to build a dam?'

'Money, power, control. Farmers crowded in to the south of us, and then the town kept growing, bringing more and more folks in. They'd get their timber from up north of here, cutting the logs and hauling them down by wagon. Jamerson saw how he could make some money and keep the town from getting much bigger at the same time, so he started charging a toll to cross his land.'

'I wondered how the toll came about.'

'But the townsfolk got smart and began floating their logs down the river, which used to run with a good strong flow. So then Jamerson dammed the river where it crossed his ranch. Now the only way back and forth is to pay the toll.'

41

'Sounds like he thought of everything.'

'And the farmers south of here can't draw much water for their crops, 'cause the dam's rigged to let just a certain amount of water go through. It's caused everybody to struggle. But it did what Jamerson wanted it to do — kept the farmers and the townsfolk down. And put money his pocket.'

'Nobody fought him on it?'

Charlie Ray snorted. 'Who's gonna do that? Farmers? Storekeepers?'

'No law out here, I suppose.'

'Nobody with a star, if that's what you mean. Each man makes his own law. And Jamerson's made his.'

'And we enforce it.'

Charlie Ray shrugged. 'It's a job. Better'n riding herd all day.'

That afternoon only a few people passed along the road. Two were from the south, so they'd already paid the toll. All Royce had to do was open the gate and let them through. Another two riders came from the north and didn't argue about the toll. Royce figured they must've gotten used to it.

Later on a freight wagon hauling some timber also came down from the north. Charlie Ray started off by charging the driver two dollars and two bits for man and wagon together.

'I paid that when I came through here from Jawbone just a week ago.'

'It's the same charge every time you go through,' said Charlie Ray. 'You know that, Walt.'

'I know it and I don't like it and neither does anybody else in these parts. And someday we're gonna do something about it!'

Charlie Ray proceeded to look over the stack of logs that filled the wagon bed. 'And twenty dollars for a full load of timber.'

The driver's face flamed with indignation. 'There's gonna be hell to pay!'

'In the meantime, pay me,' said Charlie Ray.

'How do you expect me to stay in business if I have to pay that kind of money?'

Charlie Ray shrugged. 'I don't expect anything. But I reckon you can charge that twenty dollars to whoever's buying this timber from you.'

'It's the town that's buying it.'

'The whole town?' said Royce.

'That's more than you need to know,' said Walt, giving both of them an ill-tempered look as he handed over the money. Then he slapped his team of horses into motion with the reins and spit off to the side to show his disgust.

'Twenty-two dollars and two bits,' said Charlie Ray, showing it to Royce. 'We sure made our pay today!'

He took the money into the shack, where he opened a cash box containing the day's tolls. There wasn't much in the bottom of the box.

'Not what I'd call a thriving business,' said Royce, 'if you don't count that last wagon.'

'Maybe not, but it suits Jamerson either way.' He dropped the money in and closed the lid.

Royce and Charlie Ray stayed on

duty till nearly sundown. They took the cash box with them when they headed back to the ranch, since Jamerson didn't bother to post a guard at night.

'Nobody ever sneaks through?' asked Royce as they rode along.

'Maybe, but most folks don't travel at night for fear of getting robbed by road agents.'

Royce gave a wry smile. 'Seems to me *we're* the road agents.'

Charlie Ray laughed, and the next moment a shot rang out and he fell from his horse. Instantly Royce spurred his own horse forward, just as a second shot came, and then a third. Ducking low as he galloped away, he looked back and saw two men run out from behind a low rise where they'd been waiting in ambush. They were running for Charlie Ray's horse, apparently in hopes it was the one carrying the cashbox, and they were right.

Royce wheeled his horse back around and charged them. One of the men stopped and took aim at him with a rifle. Royce drew and shot twice, killing the man. The other one by now had grabbed the reins of Charlie Ray's horse and was pulling the cash box from the saddle-bag. As Royce bore down on him, the man dropped the box and fired wildly across the saddle at Royce. Charlie Ray's horse bolted at the gunfire, leaving the man exposed. Royce shot him quickly.

The whole incident happened so fast that Royce found himself amazed when he looked around him at three dead men lying on the ground. He checked each one in turn, starting with Charlie Ray, just to be sure. But he knew dead men when he saw them. He recognized the two would-be robbers as riders who had paid the toll earlier, evidently just to get inside the fence.

The cash box had fallen open when it hit the ground. Royce gathered the money. Twenty-five dollars and six bits. The price of three men's lives.

He found two horses staked out beyond the rise where the men had hidden themselves. Then he slung all three men over their horses, tied the reins of two of the horses to the saddle horn of the one between them, and led a slow procession back to the ranch house.

It was dusk by the time he rode in. The other hands quickly gathered around, and the general hubbub brought Jamerson outside to the porch. Royce gave him a brief account of what happened, then handed him the cash box.

'Bury Charlie Ray,' said Jamerson to some of the men nearby.

Malone had sauntered up by then. 'What do we do with the others?'

A hard look came on Jamerson's face. 'Lay them out on the ground, one outside the south gate, one outside the north gate. Let the buzzards have them. That'll serve as a warning to anyone else who tries to rob me.' He turned to Royce. 'Good work, Royce. Too bad they got Charlie Ray.'

Then he went back inside the house. Malone wandered over to Royce with one of his half smiles and nodded to the dead robbers.

'You stay pretty busy, don't you?'

'Not what I expected, first day on the job.'

'It's like that sometimes. But once the word gets around, we shouldn't have any more trouble for a while. Who knows? You might even go a whole day without killing somebody.'

Lying in his bunk that night, Royce couldn't sleep. For one thing, the place on his back where Doc Haney cut into him was hurting him some. Mainly, though, he kept wondering how it was that killing had gotten so easy for him. Just draw and shoot a man and that was it. Ride off and do it again somewhere else. Sure, there was always a reason for the killing. Sometimes a good reason. But what kind of life could come from that? Where would he be ten years from now, or even five? Dead, most likely. Maybe that would be the greatest peace of all, or at least as much as he could hope for.

4

The next couple of weeks passed quietly enough. Royce and the other men working the gates alternated their duties of standing guard and riding fences and looking for trespassers who might try to cross through by cutting wire.

One afternoon Jamerson sent for Royce, who found him in his library. Malone was there, too.

'I've got a job for you and Malone. I want you to go into town. I hear some of the good citizens there are talking about incorporating, setting up a town government and hiring a marshal. They've already brought in a man named Foley.'

Royce frowned. 'Vance Foley?'

'Figured you'd know the name,' said Malone. 'A so-called 'town tamer' with his own ideas of law and order.'

'Jawbone doesn't strike me as the kind of town that needs taming,' said Royce.

'Which leads me to believe they may have other things on their minds,' said Jamerson. 'Foley's brought a couple of men with him. I want you to find out what's going on. Don't start anything, but if this Foley and his men do, I want you to be ready for it.'

'Always ready,' said Malone.

Royce said, 'If Foley's sworn in as a marshal . . . '

'That bothers you?' said Jamerson.

'Going up against the law doesn't make me comfortable.'

Jamerson smiled. 'Mark Twain said, 'A man cannot be comfortable without his own approval'. A long time ago I realized I'd never get anywhere if I only did the things I approved of. I decided to do what was necessary and approve of it later. And then be comfortable.'

Royce figured there was no reason to worry about the law until he and Malone found out what was going on in town.

As they left the house, Malone said, 'Who the deuce is Mark Twain?'

They rode south toward town, and after passing the toll gate they pulled up to look at the bones of one of the men Royce had killed. The coyotes and wolves and buzzards and ants and other vermin had all had their turn; one optimistic buzzard hopped around searching for any morsel that might've been overlooked.

'You heard of scarecrows?' said Malone. 'Well, there's no such thing as a scare-buzzard. Filthiest creatures on God's earth. The last thing I'd want when I die is to be picked over by one of them.'

And with that he pulled out his revolver and shot the buzzard, which sprawled over dead with one final flap of a crooked wing.

'Now let it be picked over by its own kind.'

Jawbone was bustling when Royce and Malone rode into town. The sound of hammering echoed down the streets, and there were more people than usual going in and out of the shops.

'I wonder what's up,' said Royce.

They rode along to where several men were putting the side of a building together, fitting the boards in place and nailing them down.

'What's that going to be?' asked Malone.

The men stopped working for a moment. One of them gave him a deliberate look square in the eyes and said, 'A jail.'

Malone laughed. 'Just what this town needs!'

'That's kind of how we figured it.'

Then the men ignored him and went back to work.

They stopped next at The Last Apache. Saloons were usually a good place for gathering rumors, if not actual facts.

'I've been wondering,' said Royce as they came to the door. 'Why'd they call it The Last Apache?'

'You didn't see the scalp hanging

over the bar? The fella who used to own this place claimed he took it off the last Apache who lived in his part of Arizona. That was before he moved up here and opened the saloon.'

'What happened to him?'

'Got shot. Turns out the scalp belonged to the next-to-the-last Apache, 'cause one day Joey One-Ear rode through and decided to rescue that scalp. Shot the owner in the course of things, then got shot himself. The new owner left the scalp where it was.'

'Who owns the place now?'

'Yale Jamerson.'

They entered the saloon, and Royce glanced above the bar. Sure enough, a long black mane of hair hung high up on the wall. The bartender was the same man who had served Royce his stew.

'What's the news, Miles?' said Malone. 'A lot of folks in town today.'

'Big meeting tonight at the Grange Hall.'

'Grange?' said Royce.

'A group of farmers,' said Malone. 'It's how they band together. I've heard there are a lot of these Granges springing up in different places, demanding things.'

'Who's going to be at this meeting?'

'Whoever wants to go,' said Miles.

'I'd like to go,' said Malone with mock enthusiasm. 'Wouldn't you, Royce?'

'Will the new marshal be there?'

'Oh, that's right,' said Miles. 'I was gonna tell you about him. He'll be there.'

Malone leaned closer on the bar. 'How about you, Miles? You gonna be there?'

'No . . . why, no. I'll be right here, working.'

'I'll be sure to tell Mr Jamerson you're taking care of business.' He turned for the door. 'Come on, Royce. Let's do some looking around.'

They walked around town trying to pick up more information, but nobody was saying much, at least not to them. Nearly everyone gave them looks that told Royce what they thought of him and Malone — two gunslingers working for the territory's boss man, helping him keep everyone under his thumb.

'Friendly little town, this Jawbone,' said Malone.

'Hard to make friends when you're squeezing money from them and holding back their water. Makes you wonder how much longer it'll last.'

'As long as Yale's guns can make it last.'

'Meaning us,' said Royce.

Malone grinned.

Deciding to wait for the evening meeting at the Grange Hall, Malone returned to The Last Apache for a drink while Royce ambled over to the General Mercantile. The inside was packed with merchandise of all descriptions, from clothes to hardware. A woman and two small children were looking through the goods. The only other people in the store were the middle-aged shopkeeper behind the counter and a younger man. When the younger one turned around,

Royce recognized Dan from the saloon fight with Blake.

'Oh, hello!' said Dan.

The shopkeeper turned around to see who was there.

'Yes, may I help you?' he said, looking Royce over and sounding less friendly than a shopkeeper should.

'Pop, this is the man who shot Blake.'

From the corner of his eye Royce saw the woman behind him hurry her children out of the store. But the shopkeeper's face softened, and he came out from behind the counter, limping a bit on a bad leg, to shake Royce's hand.

'My name's Arthur Winston. Thank you for what you did for my son.'

'He already thanked me.'

'I've told him before to stay out of saloons,' he said, shooting a dark look at Dan, who ducked his head in a futile effort to dodge the look.

'I came in for some cartridges,' said Royce, trying to get back to the business at hand.

'We have plenty of those. There's two things that always sell in a town like Jawbone. Whiskey and bullets.' He glanced at Royce's gun. 'For the Colt?'

'That's right.'

Winston pulled down a box of cartridges from a shelf of ammunition behind the counter.

'Best on the market,' he said. 'If you have any misfires, bring 'em back and we'll replace them.'

Royce nearly laughed. 'Well, sir, if they misfire on me, odds are I won't be bringing them back.'

Winston looked at him blankly for a second before realizing what he meant.

'Oh . . . I see your point.'

Dan said, 'When you drew against Blake, that was the fastest draw I've ever seen.'

His father scowled. 'Like you've seen so many men draw.'

'I've seen some.'

'Then likely you've seen men die,' said Royce. 'And that's not a good thing to see.'

He laid his money for the cartridges on the counter and left the store, wishing for a place he could go to rest. He didn't want to join Malone at the saloon. And so he headed down to Betsy's Café for an early supper.

The café was nearly empty of customers. Doc Haney was sitting at one of the tables, drinking coffee, and he waved Royce over to join him.

'Looks like you healed up well enough.'

'You did a good job,' said Royce.

'That's what I'm paid to do, though I'm not sure I'd have given you that discount if I'd known you were taking the place of the man you shot.'

'I didn't know it at the time myself.'

Betsy came over to see what Royce wanted to order, and he wondered what her attitude would be now that it was known he was working for Jamerson.

'You don't mind serving one of Jamerson's men?' he asked.

'All my life I've done one thing, and that's feed people when they're hungry.

I don't ask them what they've done or where they've been. I cook and serve, and that keeps me busy enough without mixing in other people's business. Now what do you want?'

Royce ordered pot roast. 'And some of those good biscuits of yours.'

'Always serve biscuits. And they're always good.' And with that pronouncement she went back to her kitchen at the rear of the café.

Doc Haney said, 'This town needs more people like Betsy.'

'And fewer like me.'

'Too soon to make a judgment like that. But if that's how you feel, why not ride on out?'

Royce let the question sink in and move around a little before he answered, because it was the kind of question he had asked himself many times before. Why not just ride on out, first one place, then another, and more and more after that, always riding out.

Finally he said, 'A man can't spend his life riding out of places.'

'He can if that's what he's always done.'

Royce smiled. 'You do some mind-reading on the side, Doc?'

'I only read bodies, alive and dead. If they come to me still living, I try to keep 'em that way.'

'I don't imagine many of them come to you dead.'

'You'd be wrong. People haul some poor soul in after a two hour ride in a buckboard and want me to fix him up when he's already passed on. All I can do is tell them it's too late.' He looked closely at Royce. 'And let me tell you, those are among the saddest words in this or any other language. Something to think about.'

'Right now I just want to think about biscuits.'

5

Royce lingered in the café until it was time to close. Then he headed back to The Last Apache to join up with Malone, who was finishing a low stakes poker game with two other men.

'Just in time,' said Malone, rising from the table. 'I've lost two dollars in this game.'

'Good thing you've got steady work so you can afford to lose.'

'Funny thing about that. Nobody can take my money with a gun, but they can do it easy enough with a deck of cards.'

They went on over to the Grange Hall, which was little more than a small barn with a wood floor and a collection of benches and chairs facing a low platform. Lanterns on the walls hung between the small windows. About thirty people were already there when they walked in and stood at the back.

The meeting hadn't started yet, but the babble of private discussions grew quieter as people noticed the arrival of two of Jamerson's men.

Scanning the room, Royce recognized Ludie Lundstrom from the livery stable and the man called Walt who had driven the freight wagon filled with timber. He also spotted Arthur Winston and Dan among the faces. And there was Doc Haney, sitting up front. Then Royce's eyes stopped on three men who sat off to one side. They were hard looking men who wore the face of danger and a flinty air of authority. Malone saw them, too.

'I think I'll take a seat up there,' said Malone with a touch of humor in his voice.

Malone proceeded to a chair on the opposite side of the room, directly across from the three men. Their eyes fastened on him, and he gave them a smile before slowly sitting down.

Royce still held back, looking around. It was then that he saw her, sitting on a short bench by herself, just ten feet away — the woman who woke him from a deep sleep when she knocked on the door of Jamerson's room that night. Dressed modestly, as before, she didn't look like the mistress of a man like Jamerson.

Royce told himself he needed to sit down somewhere anyway, so it might as well be over there. He eased around and sat on the bench beside her. He could tell she knew he was there, though she didn't acknowledge him.

'I see you weren't a dream after all,' said Royce in a low voice.

She glanced at him hurriedly. 'I don't know what you mean.'

'Room number four.'

'If you spread that rumor, I'll deny it,' she whispered. An anxious frown crossed her face. 'Have you said anything . . . to anyone?'

'No, and I don't plan to.'

'Good.'

He took the exchange to mean that her relationship with Jamerson was not common knowledge in the town. He glanced at her left hand. No ring, so she wasn't afraid of a husband finding out. More likely she feared the disapproval and scorn of her friends and neighbors.

'My name's Royce.' He paused, waiting. 'I could ask someone for yours.'

'Darlene Mueller,' she said tersely.

'Mueller. Like a mule. Or somebody who works with mules. Instead of muleskinners, they should call them muellers.'

She glared at him. 'And what should they call somebody who does what *you* do?'

'Considering who I work for, I wouldn't think that would trouble you.'

'It obviously doesn't trouble *you*.'

'What's obvious isn't always what it seems. I learned that as a kid when I tried to walk across a frozen lake and fell through.'

'Maybe you didn't learn the lesson well enough,' she said.

Their conversation ended abruptly

when an older man with white side whiskers stepped on to the platform and called for everyone's attention.

'I see some new faces tonight, so for those who don't know me, I'm Zachary Phelps, president of the bank here in town. Most of you are aware that Jawbone has been struggling the last couple of years, trying to grow, but held back by . . . well, let's say circumstances.'

'Let's say Jamerson!' yelled someone in the crowd, which came now to about fifty men and a few women.

'It doesn't matter what name you put on it,' said Phelps. 'The fact is, we're a regular town and we need civil ordinances.'

A loud murmur of approval rose from the crowd.

'Right now we're in the process of putting up a jail, which is costing more than it should because every load of timber coming down from the north is getting taxed. I call it a tax, because that's what it amounts to.'

'Robbery's another name for it,' came a voice, followed by shouts of agreement.

'All right, all right,' said Phelps. 'Call it what you will, but if there's going to be any taxing of the people, it should be voted on by the people. And if anyone tries to make up his own taxes, then law officers hired by the people should see to it that such unlawful activity is stopped!'

General applause broke out. Royce looked at Malone, who seemed to be having a good time, grinning at the commotion. Phelps continued.

'Over the last few weeks we passed around a petition, signed by most of the folks here tonight. Acting on that petition, we formed a town council and sent for a professional lawman. He's here tonight, so let me go ahead and introduce Vance Foley.'

Foley stood up, all six foot two of him, with a black mustache and a barrel chest. He strode on to the platform to stand beside Phelps.

'Mr Phelps said it plain, but let me

make it plainer. Your town council makes the laws. I go out and make those laws stick, no matter who likes it or doesn't like it. I've brought two deputies with me — Jake Hawthorne and Tom Pratt.'

The two men stood up to show themselves to the crowd.

'These men are battle-tested,' said Foley, 'and they've ridden with me through many a town. Whatever we need to do, we'll do.'

Having made his statement, he went back and sat down with his men.

'I'm confident,' said Phelps, 'that Marshal Foley and his deputies will vigorously apply the laws within our jurisdiction.'

Malone stood up. 'Which raises a question, if you don't mind.'

Phelps hesitated as the crowd stirred. Everyone knew Malone.

'If you've got something to say, go ahead,' said Phelps.

'Just how far does this new 'jurisdiction' go? I mean, does it stop where the town stops? At the last building?'

'No,' said Phelps. 'The jurisdiction extends to whatever affects the town.'

Malone raised his eyebrows. 'That's an awful lot of territory. And this petition, did everyone get a chance to sign it? Everyone in the 'jurisdiction', I mean? I know I didn't. And I'm pretty sure Mr Jamerson didn't, though I'm altogether sure he'll have something to say about it.'

Phelps raised a defiant chin, his white whiskers bristling. 'You can tell your boss that the law has come to Jawbone. And when the law has something to say to him, it'll be said in writing first, and later in person if necessary.'

The crowd applauded and people yelled, 'That's right!' and 'You tell him!'

Malone smiled again. 'By 'in person' you mean by these gentlemen here?' He nodded toward Foley and his men.

'Exactly,' said Phelps.

'If they want to talk to Mr Jamerson, that's just fine. Of course, they'll have to pay the toll when they ride through.'

Foley rose to his feet, followed by Hawthorne and Pratt. Royce had been watching Malone have his fun, but suddenly things were turning serious, so he also rose to his feet, drawing the attention of Foley and his men. Everyone in the hall grew quiet, and Darlene pulled farther away from Royce.

The five men faced each over the heads of the crowd. Each man's hand hung ready by his gun. The air tingled with a sharp expectancy, the way it did just before a lightning strike.

Royce broke the tension.

'Banker Phelps, I suggest you pass an ordinance against any gunplay in the Grange Hall. Come on, Malone. We need to ride.'

Malone made his way back toward Royce, keeping an eye on Foley. The crowd relaxed a little.

Then Malone spoke one final time. 'Don't forget to give these lawmen badges to wear over their hearts. Nothing beats a bright, shiny target.'

Royce backed out of the hall, followed by Malone. As soon as they were outside, Malone started complaining.

'That really burns my hide. They're gonna pin a star on Foley and call him a lawman, but he's just another hired gun.'

'From what I hear, he's a good one.'

'Being good's not the same as being the best.'

'You're saying you're the best?'

'You've never seen me shoot. But I've seen you. And yeah, I'm saying I'm the best.'

'Tell me that again after you've seen Foley shoot.'

'I will.'

They rode back to the ranch to tell Jamerson what was going on and found him sitting on the porch with his wife. A lamp glowed on the small table between them, while a three-quarter moon brightened the landscape beyond the range of the lamplight.

'Good evening, Mrs Jamerson,' said Royce.

'Good evening,' she replied, then turned a questioning glance to her husband.

'Will you excuse us, Sarah?' said Jamerson.

'Of course.' She rose and went quietly into the house.

Jamerson waited until she was inside, then said, 'You were gone long enough. What did you find out?'

Malone gave a detailed account of the meeting, stressing his contempt for the new lawmen. When he was done, Jamerson turned to Royce.

'And how do you see it?'

Royce drew in some of the night air and held it a second, because he didn't want to say what he knew to be the case. Finally he spoke.

'If you don't give in, there'll be a gun battle. We'll kill the lawmen or they'll kill us, and maybe you. Either way, men will die. You have to figure whether you're ready to take it that far.'

Jamerson seemed to think it over. 'There's just three of them and there's not even a court or a judge in Jawbone.'

'I don't think they're going to wait for one,' said Malone. 'They've hired these men to break you.'

'I don't break that easy,' said Jamerson. 'But they haven't tried anything yet, so for now we'll sit back and wait for their next move. You said they're planning to give me a notice of some kind, in writing.'

'According to the banker, Phelps,' said Royce.

'Fine. Let them do it.'

'And then what?' said Malone.

'Then I'll give them my answer, written in blood.'

6

The next morning Royce was up early. He sat on a corral fence and waited for the sunrise, so far just a rim of white on the eastern plain. Other than the twitch of the horses and the half-hearted crow of a rooster, everything was still. Then a solitary figure walked slowly by, twenty feet away.

'Mornin',' said Royce quietly.

Mrs Jamerson jumped a little, startled out of her reverie.

'Who's there? Oh, it's you, Royce.'

'Yes, ma'am. Didn't mean to scare you.'

'You didn't. Not really. Not as much as some things do.' She gazed toward the house and didn't move.

'What is it that scares you?'

She looked around at him and moved a little closer. 'Ambition. And what it leads to.'

'I wouldn't know. I've never had any.'

Her face become more defined as she approached in the hazy light. 'You never wanted to make a place for yourself?'

'I guess I figured I'd find one somewhere, if I wandered around long enough.'

'Yale says a man only gets what he's willing to take. I wonder sometimes about the value of what gets taken, and whether it's worth what a man loses by taking it.'

She fell into a silence then, and Royce didn't break it. After a few moments she looked toward the sunrise, now a golden band on the horizon.

'Beautiful, isn't it?'

'Every time,' said Royce.

'I remember the sunrises when Yale and I first came out here. The world was new for us then, and every dawn was a promise that every wonderful dream would come true. Some dreams did. Most didn't.'

'Has it always been just the two of you?'

'You mean did we have any children? I had two miscarriages, and that was all I could do. Yale never said so, but I know he took it hard that he never had a son . . . that I could never give him one.'

'Maybe you took it harder than he did.'

'Strange, the things a man and wife share . . . and the things they don't, or can't.'

The dawn was on her face now, illuminating the lines and the weariness there. She turned back toward the house.

'Be careful today, Royce,' she said without looking around.

'Yes, ma'am.'

He watched her until she disappeared into the house, and he wondered if she knew about Darlene Mueller. Probably so. That sort of thing would be hard to keep secret in a town like Jawbone. On the other hand, Darlene had made it sound like no one else knew about her backstairs relationship with Jamerson.

Royce shrugged the whole thing off. Whatever it was, it was no concern of his, he told himself. And yet thoughts of Darlene still lingered.

Jamerson assigned both Royce and Malone to the south toll gate that day. If trouble was coming, it would have to get past them. They settled down in chairs inside the shack where the window gave them a clear view of the road toward town. Malone seemed in good spirits.

'My, oh my, I do hope Marshal Foley and his boys are wearing their big shiny badges when they come.'

'Gunplay with the law isn't a good idea if it can be avoided,' said Royce.

'You do the avoiding, and I'll do the gunplay. You notice nobody calls it gun 'work.' It's gun 'play.' And it makes me come alive.'

'Someday it might have the opposite effect.'

Malone laughed. 'Then I'll die with a smile, doing what I like.' He gave Royce a curious look then. 'For a man in your

76

chosen profession, you don't seem too settled with the actual doing of it.'

'A man can be good at something without enjoying it.'

'Sure, but what a waste.'

'As for choosing this profession, it was more like it chose me.'

'How'd that happen?'

Royce hesitated, because telling stories from the past didn't come easily to him. But the tedium of sitting and waiting inside the shack had worked on him to the point he didn't mind talking.

'Two brothers had it in for me, back when I was barely seventeen. There was no real reason behind it. Somehow we just rubbed each other the wrong way. I think they had kin fighting for the North, but that's how it was with lots of folks in Missouri — some taking one side, some another. I had fist fights with one or the other of these boys for a year or more, off and on. Then the war ended, my mother died, and the boys' uncle made me an offer on the land. It was sixty acres, right next to his. I told him no. The boys were eighteen and nineteen then, and they started wearing guns. They kept after me, firing random shots in my direction, making all kinds of threats. So I put on a gun myself. And I practiced. And practiced. And practiced some more. One day in town they saw me wearing the gun, and they called me out. I suppose they thought I'd be easy pickings and then their uncle could get the land. I stood there waiting for them to make a move. And when they did, I shot and killed them both.' He stopped.

'And?'

'Then I sold the land to somebody else and started riding. And kept on riding.'

Malone mulled this over for a minute. 'You say you didn't choose this profession. But you put on the gun. You practiced with it. You wore it to town. You faced the brothers. You shot them dead. And you went away to take more jobs using your gun. Sure sounds to me like you chose the profession.'

Royce slowly shook his head. 'I wouldn't choose it again.'

'You're fooling yourself. Every time you take a job with a Yale Jamerson, you make that same choice. You know you do.'

He couldn't deny the logic, but he couldn't accept it, either. And what was the point in even thinking about it? Whatever he had become, and however he had gotten there, he didn't see any way to change it now.

A lazy couple of hours passed, then Royce spotted dust rising far down the road.

'Someone's coming.'

They both stepped out into the sunlight and waited. A lone rider approached: it was Phelps, the banker. He reined in his horse, unfazed by the sight of Royce and Malone, as if he had expected nothing less.

'Well, now, Mr Phelps,' said Malone. 'Is it a bank holiday?'

'I'm not coming as a banker. I'm coming as a representative of the town council to serve notice on Jamerson.'

Royce said, 'We thought Marshal Foley would be the one doing the serving.'

'It may come to that later. Now let me through.'

'Sure,' said Malone. 'Right after you pay the toll.'

'That's outrageous! I'm not traveling through to the north. I'm going to see Jamerson.'

Malone grinned. 'That's just fine. Four bits.'

Phelps blustered and fumed, but finally he reached in his pocket and tossed him the money.

'Now open the gate!'

Royce swung it open for him, and Phelps spurred his horse forward. It was a more aggressive spurring than his horse was used to, and Phelps nearly lost his seating as he galloped through.

Malone headed for his own horse as Royce closed the gate.

'I'm not missing this. Come on.'

'What about the tolls?' said Royce.

'I've got the banker's four bits, and

that's all there's been today. We'll send somebody else back to watch the gate.'

Together they rode to the ranch house, deliberately staying behind Phelps until they got there, then catching up with him as he dismounted. He watched them warily as he knocked six fast times on the door. Mrs Jamerson opened it.

'Why, Mr Phelps, how nice of you to call.'

'Not to mention expensive,' he said, glancing at Malone. 'Is your husband in?'

'He's in the study. Go right in.'

Phelps entered the book-lined study, followed by Royce and Malone. Jamerson looked up from the paperwork he was doing, but didn't rise.

'Hello, Phelps. I see you have an escort.'

'And I see you're going over your books.'

'You have a banker's eye.'

'Don't forget to add in my fifty cents.'

81

Jamerson leaned back in his chair. 'Sit if you want to. No charge.'

'I don't need to sit. I just need to give you this.'

He brought out a folded document from the inside pocket of his coat and handed it to Jamerson, who held it without opening it.

'Who wrote it?'

Phelps squared himself. 'I did.'

'Then you tell me what it says.'

'Gladly. In brief, it's an ordinance that forbids the charging of tolls and damming of the river. You've been given notice to open the road to traffic and to let the river flow unimpeded.'

Jamerson set the document down. 'Is it the town's water?'

'It's . . . it's God's water!'

'It may be God's water, but it's my dam. If the town needs more water, that can be arranged. For a price.'

Phelps turned redder in the face than he already was. 'We're not paying for what's rightly ours.'

'Yes, you will. Or I may shut off the

water completely.'

'Even you wouldn't do that. What if somebody farther upriver did the same to you? What would you do then?'

'That's not the question. The question is, what are you going to do?'

'The town has already done it. We've brought in the law.'

'So I've heard.' He got to his feet. 'Now let me tell you something. You'll need a lot more law than what you've got if you expect to give me orders.'

Jamerson picked up the unread document and tore it in pieces.

'Very well,' said Phelps. 'You've been warned. You're forcing me to turn the matter over to Marshal Foley.'

'The only thing I'm forcing you to do is get off my land. Now.'

Scowling, Phelps turned without a word and went striding from the room and out the front door.

'He believes his man Foley can do the job,' said Jamerson. 'But he's wrong.'

'Dead wrong,' said Malone.

'I'm wondering what Foley will try first,' said Royce. 'You have to assume he's no fool.'

'Be on the watch. And stay on the south gate, both of you. When Foley comes, make him sorry that he did.'

Royce knew exactly what he meant and didn't take it with the same good cheer as Malone.

7

For the next week everything was quiet. Occasional traffic on the road started again as people saw there was no immediate confrontation. Then one day through the open window of the shack Royce saw a number of riders coming.

'This may be it,' he said, getting to his feet.

'How many?'

'Four.'

Malone laughed. 'Maybe old Phelps is coming with them.'

They stepped out to the gate. The riders were close enough now to see their faces, but neither Foley nor his men were among them.

'Nope,' said Malone. 'Just another two dollars coming up the road.'

The riders pulled up, four abreast. They were hardscrabble-looking men — dusty and dirty.

'What's with the gate?' said one of them.

'Toll road from this point on,' said Malone. 'Four bits each.'

'What if we can't pay?' said another.

'Then you have to turn back.'

The men were taking the measure of Royce and Malone, looking them over. Then the first one spoke again, addressing the other three.

'Well, boys, we can't go back now. Might as well give these fellas what they're asking for.'

And with that all four of them went for their guns. Instantly Malone's gun was up and firing, with Royce's close behind. Two men fell from their horses, but the other two kept shooting as their horses frantically shied away. Malone ducked to the left and Royce to the right during the rapid exchange of gunfire. One rider slumped over in the saddle, struck by Royce's bullet, and his horse ran away with him down the road. Malone finished the fourth man, then leapt to the gate, took aim, and sent one final shot into the wounded man on horseback. The rider jumped at the impact and slid off his horse.

As Malone calmly reloaded his gun, he looked over at Royce.

'Now you've seen me draw.'

'I wasn't paying that much attention,' said Royce. 'I was kinda busy at the time.'

Malone laughed. 'We make a good team.'

'Good enough for this day.'

They opened the gate and went out to the men they had killed. Malone dug into the pants pockets of one and pulled out some money.

'See? He did have enough for the toll.' He slipped the money in his own pocket.

'What's that about?' said Royce.

'What? The money? Well, he sure doesn't need it now. He probably stole it in the first place, and who would I return it to?' Then Malone reached into the man's shirt pocket. 'What's this? Well, looky here.'

Royce saw the star in his hand. 'A badge?'

'Let's check the others.'

The other three also carried concealed badges. Each one said 'Deputy'.

'Handy things to have,' said Royce, 'especially when you set out for a killing.'

'Somebody must keep a supply of these.'

'Somebody named Foley.'

'The gutless man hired these fellas to jump us,' said Malone.

'Smarter than coming himself, knowing we'd be looking for him. Let's go tell Jamerson.'

'Just a minute,' said Malone, bending over to wipe his polished boots with a handkerchief. He looked back up and smiled. 'Killing is dusty work.'

They went and got their instructions from Jamerson, and an hour later they were headed into Jawbone with four bodies piled in a wagon. Royce was driving, with Malone riding alongside.

'I've been thinking,' said Royce, 'that

if Foley sends a lot more men our way, it might take more than just the two of us.'

Malone grunted. 'There's nobody else at the YJ who's all that good with a gun. Blake was the closest, and you made short work of him. Most of the boys are like these four saddle tramps, and in a fight they'd likely end up the same way. On the other hand, at least they'd provide more targets to draw fire away from us.'

Royce smiled grimly at Malone's reasoning. But he couldn't deny the practical truth of it.

As soon as they pulled into Jawbone, they drew immediate attention. People stepped into the street to look, then stepped away again, wanting to see what was going on, but not wanting to get involved in it. Royce pulled up on the brace of horses and stopped right in front of the new jail, completed now. Then he and Malone went inside.

Foley was sitting alone at a desk, just outside a doorway leading back to two empty cells. When he looked up and saw who was coming in, his face betrayed surprise.

Royce said, 'Marshal, we'd like to report a case of attempted murder.'

'Whose?'

'Ours,' said Malone. 'But notice it was only 'attempted'. I'm sure you're relieved to hear the attempt failed.'

'What happened?'

'Four men tried to kill us at the south toll gate,' said Royce.

'Is that so? Who were they?'

Malone said, 'We thought maybe you knew.'

'How would I know that? So what happened? You drove them off?'

'No,' said Royce. 'We drove them in. They're laid out in the wagon outside.'

Foley rose quickly to his feet and went out to the street, where several people had gathered to gawk. They backed away as Foley came up.

'You killed four men?'

'Four attempted murderers,' said Malone. 'Strictly self-defense.'

'You want to claim the bodies?' asked Royce.

Foley considered his answer. 'Why should *I* claim them? Take them down to the undertaker's.'

Royce climbed up on the seat of the wagon and took the reins as Foley retreated to his doorway, watching. Malone mounted up and waited till Royce was driving away before he looked back at Foley.

'Oh, Marshal, I nearly forgot to give you something. Maybe you can find some use for these.'

He pulled out the four deputy badges and tossed them at Foley's feet.

'Imagine the gall of those fellas, impersonating the law that way.'

Then he grinned and rode off, leaving Foley to stare grimly down at the badges.

They left the bodies with the undertaker, who wanted to know who was going to pay for the burying. Royce told him to send the bill to the marshal's office.

'Now that we've taken care of that,' said Malone, 'I'm heading for The Last Apache.'

'Go ahead. As long as I have the wagon, I might as well see if Jamerson's order of barbed wire has come in.'

But it wasn't just the wire that was drawing him to the General Mercantile. When he was driving into town, he had seen Darlene Mueller watching as the wagon passed, and she had turned away into the store.

Darlene was talking with Dan when Royce entered. They stopped talking when they saw him.

'Hello,' said Dan, but it wasn't as friendly as before.

'Hello. Can you tell me if you've got Jamerson's wire yet?'

'I'll have to check with Pa. He's out back.'

Dan left, and Darlene remained silent, trying not to look at him.

'Good to see you again, Miss Mueller.'

Her eyes sparked. 'It wasn't good to

see you, bringing in a wagon load of corpses. What happened? Did they refuse to pay the toll?'

'They tried to pay, all right. With lead.'

'I'm sure Jamerson was very pleased with the outcome.'

'If you feel that way about Jamerson, I don't understand why you, well, you know.'

'No, I don't know, and you don't, either.'

Royce couldn't figure her out. He decided to change the subject.

'Shopping, are you?'

'I'm sure you'll laugh, but I was finding out how much it would cost to order one hundred hymnals.'

'Hymnals.' No, he certainly couldn't figure her out. 'I didn't know Jawbone had a church.'

'It doesn't. But we're going to build one someday if we can ever get the lumber for it.'

'What does the preacher say about it?'

'We don't have a preacher.'

'No preacher.'

'We figured it would be easier to get a preacher if we had a ready-made church to put him in.'

'With hymnals.'

'Oh, I know it sounds silly. Especially to someone like you.'

'No, I think a church is a fine thing . . . though it's hard to recall the last time I was in one.'

'I'm not surprised,' she said, and with a quick turn walked out of the store.

A moment later Dan reappeared.

'Nope. Hasn't come in yet. Maybe next week.'

'It's brought in from the south, I take it?'

'Like all the other shipments,' said Dan.

'Everything but lumber.'

'No trees to speak of down that way for more miles than I've ever seen. Lucky for the town Jamerson doesn't own the land south of here, too.'

'Miss Mueller sounds like she doesn't

care much for Mr Jamerson.'

'Nobody does, if you don't mind my saying so.'

'I don't mind,' said Royce. 'About Miss Mueller . . . being the attractive woman she is, I'm surprised she's still a 'Miss' and not a 'Missus' by now.'

'It's not that she hasn't been asked. But she's kinda picky.'

'Picky,' he repeated, questioning how true that could be if she'd taken up with Jamerson.

'That's right. Darlene has a mind and a half of her own.'

'You're on first name terms with her?'

'Why shouldn't I be?' said Dan. 'She's my sister.'

'Your sister!'

'You didn't know?'

Royce stood still a moment, trying to figure this out. 'Does she work here with you?'

'No, she's got her own little shop down the street where she sews clothes — makes new clothes and patches old.

A lot of folks can't afford new bought, but they'll pay to fix what's torn. Especially men who never learned to sew.'

Royce nodded, then said, 'Mueller.'

'What?'

'Her last name's Mueller, not Winston like yours.'

Dan looked like he was going to say something, but his father came in at that moment.

'Oh, hello,' said Winston. 'Did Dan tell you about the wire?'

'Yes, he told me. Nothing to do but wait for it, I suppose.'

With a final nod to father and son, Royce left the store, but with more than wire on his mind.

8

The next day Jamerson called for Royce and Malone to ride with him up to the dam. As the three of them rode along, he let them know how he planned to respond to the town's order to rescind the tolls.

'I'm going to double them,' he said.

Malone laughed. 'That'll stir things up.'

'Nobody will pay that much,' said Royce. 'You'll end up losing money.'

'I don't care about the money. If the town wants a showdown, then let's get on with it. We'll force Foley's hand and after he's gone, the town will give up.'

'And if they don't?' said Malone.

'That's what I want to show you.'

For the first time Royce saw the dam up close, and he was surprised by the size of it. Two hundred feet long, twenty feet high, and ten feet thick, it was constructed of tightly connected logs in a way Royce had never seen before. It blocked the river channel and backed the water up into a wide lake on the north side, while a small opening near the base of the dam allowed a modest flow of water to pass through to the south.

'That's some piece of work,' said Royce.

'Sure ain't no beaver dam,' said Malone.

'It was designed by an engineer I brought out here from back East,' said Jamerson. 'Cost me plenty, but it's been worth it.'

For a moment, sitting on his horse and surveying his realm, Jamerson seemed almost content. Cattle grazed nearby, and ducks swam in and out of the reeds that had sprung up along the edge of the lake.

'We'll see what the town does about the new toll,' said Jamerson. 'If they back down, fine. If not, the next thing I do is shut off the water.'

'You can do that?' asked Royce.

'I had it built so I could. All I have to do is close that gate over there.'

Royce saw there was a thick door set just above the opening in the dam. Lowered into place, it would seal the dam entirely.

'That would dry up the town plenty fast,' said Malone. 'And the farmers, too.'

Royce turned to Jamerson. 'Leaving Foley out of it, what exactly do you want from the town?'

'It's more what I don't want. I don't want the town to keep on getting bigger, crowding me with their so-called civilization. I want things to stay how they were when I first built up this place.' He took a breath of the prairie wind, as if calling back the scent of yesterday. 'A writer named Thoreau said, 'The mass of men lead lives of quiet desperation.' But I'm not one of those men, and I refuse to let anyone make me into that. This land will not be overrun with farmers and merchants.'

Royce had heard such talk before, in many other places. 'It's hard to hold back time.'

Jamerson grunted. 'It's a wise man who knows his limitations, and a fool who thinks he doesn't have any.'

'Who said that?' asked Malone.

'I did. I know I can't hold back the future forever. But I can hold it back for as long as I'm still here.'

They dismounted at the dam and climbed up one end of it. Walking along the top, Jamerson stopped when he got to the middle and showed them how to reach down and release a lever that would cause the heavy door to fall into place by simple gravity.

'I'm showing you this,' said Jamerson, 'because when the time comes, I want men I can trust to handle the job. Not just to shoot whoever tries to stop you, but to get this dam closed. People out here are touchy when it comes to water, and I know a lot of my men didn't like the idea of this dam in the first place. Malone, I know I can count on you. Royce . . . ' He regarded him with the same kind of appraising look he gave him that first night in The Last Apache. 'I'm trusting you won't have any qualms about carrying out my order.'

Royce knew what to say and how to say it. 'As long as I'm working for you, Mr Jamerson, I'll do what you tell me to do.'

Jamerson nodded, satisfied with his answer.

Later that day Royce rode into Jawbone with a hand-lettered sign that Jamerson told him to post somewhere in town. He figured outside the marshal's office would be a good place, so he got off his horse, unrolled the sign, took out four small nails he'd brought along for the purpose, and with the butt of his gun tacked the sign to the front of the jail, next to the door.

Foley heard the tapping and came out.

'What's going on?'

'Just putting up a public notice,

101

Marshal. This is a public building, isn't it?'

He looked at the sign, which said: ALL TOLLS NOW DOUBLE — Yale Jamerson.

'Does Jamerson really think the town will stand for this?'

'No, Marshal, he doesn't.'

Foley took a moment to look Royce over and take his measure.

'You know, one of those four men you brought in yesterday was shot in the back. Did you shoot him?'

'Not in the back.'

'You have any witnesses to the shooting?'

'Sure. Malone.'

'Was Malone the one who shot him in the back?'

'You'd have to ask Malone. Any idea why they drew down on us?'

'You'd have to ask them.'

'They're pretty tight-lipped,' said Royce.

Foley allowed himself a slow smile. 'I guess we could go on like this all day.'

'That would be an awful waste of time,' said Royce. Then he nodded at the sign. 'I'm sure you'll help spread the word.'

'The word'll get spread. Don't worry about that.'

'I don't worry about anything,' said Royce, mounting his horse.

'Too bad. You should.'

Royce kept an eye on Foley as he rode on down the street, relaxing only after he turned down an alley and came around toward Darlene's shop on the next street over. He stopped a minute and took a shirt from his saddle-bag. Grasping it at one shoulder, he pulled on the upper sleeve and ripped the stitches open about two inches. Then he rode on to the shop.

When he walked in, Darlene was showing some embroidery to a woman in a plain, faded dress. Darlene glanced up briefly, looked annoyed, and then ignored him.

'It's very fine work,' said the woman. 'But it just doesn't suit me. I wish I could wear something like that. I truly do. But no . . . I can't. Thank you, though, for showing it to me.'

'Anytime, Mrs Warren.'

The woman turned away with obvious reluctance, but then spotted Royce and hastened her step as she left the shop. Royce wished for a second he didn't always have that effect.

Darlene said, 'I hope you're not here to scare away my customers.'

'More likely your prices scared her away.'

'What is it you want?'

'I hear you fix torn clothing.' He held out the shirt. 'The sleeve pulled loose.'

She took it from him. 'I thought maybe you had a bullet hole in it.'

'Then I'd need sewing, too, and I'd be over at the Doc's instead of here.'

She needed only a second to study the problem. 'This won't be hard to sew up. You can come back for it tomorrow.'

'Couldn't you do it now while I wait? Truth is, I don't have that many shirts.'

'All right. But it's fifty cents.'

104

'Fifty cents! To sew a shirt?'

'Same as it costs to ride through the Jamerson ranch.'

Royce grinned, both at her remark and because he wasn't going to tell her the toll was double now.

'OK,' he said. 'Fifty cents.'

She stood looking at him, waiting. He reached in his pocket and handed over the fifty cents. Silently she took out a needle and thread and scissors and went to work. He watched her hands and fingers moving quickly, skillfully.

'You don't seem to like me very much,' said Royce.

Her hands slowed for a moment. 'I don't know why I should.'

'Your brother never told you what happened?'

'In the saloon? Of course I heard about it. But what you did, you didn't do for Dan. You didn't even know him then.'

'So why do you think I did it?'

She looked up at him. 'All right, I'll tell you. I think it was just a matter of two hungry dogs fighting to the death, simply because that's their nature. One eats the other.'

Royce paused, momentarily shocked. 'Actually, I had stew that night.'

Darlene went back to sewing, and he said nothing more. But he was sorry she felt that way about him, and he wondered if part of what she said was true.

After another minute or so, she tied off the thread. 'This will hold for a long time.'

He looked at the shirt and could hardly see where it had been mended. 'You're good at what you do. Do you like doing it?'

'Not especially.'

'You just do it for the money. The way I work for Jamerson.'

'Some things I wouldn't do for money.'

'For love, then?' Because hadn't they first met when she came to Jamerson's room above the saloon?

Darlene gave him a strange look. 'I

don't know what you're talking about.'

'I'm not sure I do, cither.' He turned to leave, then looked back. 'But I know this much. Next time I tear a shirt, I'll stop by the General Mercantile and buy a needle and thread.'

After packing the shirt away in his saddle-bag, Royce was just about to mount up when a voice called out.

'You — Royce!'

He turned to see Tom Pratt, one of Foley's deputies, coming toward him from across the street. So he waited.

'The marshal's got some questions for you.'

'Sorry. I'm fresh out of answers.'

By now Pratt was standing right beside him, eye to eye.

'I'll drag you over there if I have to.'

'You have to.'

Pratt swung a fast punch toward Royce's head with all the assurance of someone who had done such things successfully many times before. This time he caught air as Royce slipped underneath and came up with a hard fist to Pratt's midsection and another to the side of his head. But Pratt wasn't going down that easily. He struck back furiously, and the two men traded a series of quick punches, each blow doing its damage until finally Pratt sank down on one knee.

Suddenly a hand grabbed Royce's shoulder and spun him around in time to catch a blow from Jake Hawthorne, the other deputy. Royce fell backward over Pratt, and the three men together flailed and struck and grunted till Royce kicked Pratt away and scrambled up to beat Hawthorne back. Then Pratt was on him again, but Royce sent him away choking with an elbow to the throat, just before Hawthorne swung once more, catching him on the jaw. Royce staggered, but threw his open left hand into Hawthorne's charging face, followed by a straight right that sent Hawthorne reeling.

'That's enough!' boomed a voice.

Foley stood a few feet away with a shotgun leveled at Royce. The three of them stood panting from their exertions until Foley spoke again.

'Take his gun, Jake.'

Hawthorne pulled Royce's Colt from his holster. As Royce picked up his hat, he noticed his shirt had gotten ripped in the fight. He also saw Darlene had come out of her shop and was standing by the door, watching.

'Well,' he said with a slight grin and a tug at his shirt, 'lucky for me I've got a spare.'

'You're under arrest, Royce,' said Foley.

'What's the charge?'

'Assault and battery.'

'I call it self-defense.'

'It doesn't matter what you call it. Only what I call it. And I call it assaulting a peace officer.'

'He didn't seem all that peaceful to me,' said Royce.

Pratt pushed him from behind. 'Go on.'

They marched him over to the jail and locked him in a cell. It wasn't the first cell Royce had been in, but the first one in a long time.

'What happens now?' he asked.

'Nothing happens now,' said Foley. 'When it does happen, you'll find out about it then.'

After that, Foley left him alone. His cuts and bruises from the fight began to bother him now that everything had calmed down. He stretched out on the bunk, which was actually pretty comfortable; after all, the whole place was new. As he lay there, he wondered what Jamerson would do when he found out about this. Would he just leave him here? Or would he come for him? There was no use guessing about it, so Royce did what he hadn't done in years: he took a nap.

He was awakened a short time later by Doc Haney's voice outside in the marshal's office. Listening quietly and catching a glimpse through the bars, he could tell Haney was patching up Pratt and Hawthorne.

'They gonna be all right?' said Foley.

'Sure, sure. Nothing to worry about,' said Haney.

Pratt said, 'You wouldn't say that if you were the one doing the bleeding.'

'You're not bleeding any more. All you need is some rest.'

'Is my nose broken?' asked Hawthorne.

'It looks broken, but it wasn't broken today,' said Haney. 'And now I better take a look at your prisoner.'

'Let him rot,' said Pratt.

'This way,' said Foley.

A moment later Foley brought the doctor in, unlocked the cell, then locked it again with Haney inside before going out.

'Royce, you look a mess.'

'A good thing jail cells don't come with mirrors.'

'You hurt anywhere besides your head? Ribs, maybe?'

'No, I'm OK.'

'Take off your shirt anyway. I want to see my handiwork from that pellet I took out of you.'

Royce did as he was instructed while Haney poured some alcohol on a wad of cotton.

'First let me clean up that face.'

He dabbed at Royce's wounded flesh with the alcohol, making him wince.

'Curious thing about alcohol,' said Haney. 'Men have no problem putting it inside of them, but they flinch when it goes on the outside.'

'Too bad it's not the other way around.'

'Amen to that. Turn around and let me see that back.'

Royce turned and heard Haney rummaging in his bag.

'Well? How's it look?'

'Hold still.'

With tweezers Haney pulled out the last fragments of the stitches.

'It looks fine,' he said, 'though you should've come in sooner to let me take the stitches out.'

'I didn't come in *this* time. And next time I need to get sewed on, I might have Miss Mueller do it instead.'

'She can sew up wounds when I start sewing dresses. You interested in her sewing?'

'I was today.' He turned back around. 'That reminds me. I've got a shirt in my saddle-bag I sure could use, but my horse is over by Darlene's shop.'

'I'll look into it,' said Haney. 'I notice you went pretty fast from 'Miss Mueller' to 'Darlene'. What does she think about that?'

'Not much so far. And I still don't understand why she's Mueller if her father is Winston.'

'The way I heard it, she took her mother's name for some reason. That was long before I came to town. Arthur Winston's wife died giving birth to Dan. That was also before I got here, I hasten to add. So many women get pregnant without my help, but as soon as the baby's due, that's when they want me.'

'That's the only part they're willing to pay you for.'

'Hah!' Haney shook his head as he

113

closed up his bag. 'By the way, you never did tell me how you got that pellet in you in the first place.'

'I got bushwhacked by somebody who wanted me out of the way. Getting thrown in jail is better than that, I suppose.'

'Maybe you should find a less hazardous occupation.'

Royce smiled. 'I hear there's an opening for a preacher.'

Haney called for the marshal to let him out, and Royce was sorry to see him go. But less than an hour later Foley ushered Darlene into the jail area: she was carrying his shirt.

'You can talk,' said Foley, 'but I'm not letting you into the cell.'

'I don't want to go in,' said Darlene.

Royce stood up as Foley left them alone. She handed him his shirt through the bars.

'Here. Doc said you needed it, and he was busy.'

'And you weren't?'

'He turned your horse over to Axel at the stable.'

'That's good. And thank you for the shirt.'

Royce slipped off the torn and bloody shirt he was wearing. Darlene fidgeted a little as he stood barechested in front of her.

'I didn't mean to make you uncomfortable,' he said.

'Being in a jail is what makes me uncomfortable.'

'Me, too.' He put on the freshly mended shirt and fastened the front. 'Now I feel better.'

'Give me the other one,' she said. 'I might as well stitch that one, too.'

He hesitated. 'It's got blood on it. Some of it may even be mine.'

'I've washed bloody shirts before.'

'I'm not sure I can afford your prices.'

'Oh, just give it here.'

He smiled and handed her the shirt. 'It may take a little more patching than this one did.'

'Let me worry about that. It'll be ready for you when you get out of jail.'

'Whenever that might be. And that reminds me. I don't know if anyone's told Jamerson where I am. Is there any way you could get a message to him?'

'No,' she snapped. 'I don't want anything to do with him. And if you weren't in that cell, I wouldn't have anything to do with you, either.'

Then with his shirt flapping in her hand, she stalked back through the marshal's office and out the door.

9

It was the next day before Malone showed up looking for Royce, grinning as he came back to the cell.

'This is the first time I ever visited a jail cell of my own free will.'

Royce noticed his holster was empty. 'What happened to your six-gun?'

'The marshal offered to hold it for me while I came in to say hello. When he gives it back, I'll be sure to count the bullets.'

'So Jamerson finally noticed I didn't make it back last night.'

'We noticed,' said Malone. 'Figured you were either dead, in jail, or laid up with a woman somewhere. Whichever one it was, there was no point in rushing to find out.'

'Thanks. So what now?'

'You're gonna be a trailblazer for the new legal system around here. Now that they've got a marshal who has started arresting people — people meaning you — they gotta have a trial. And for a trial they need a judge. The town's bringing in a circuit judge to settle the case. He'll be here at the end of the week, so you've only got to stay locked up a few more days.'

'Unless the judge decides I need to stay a whole lot longer.'

'Here's something else. No lawyers in this town, so Yale's going to be your lawyer.'

'What does Jamerson know about defending people in court?'

'About as much as this town knows about putting people on trial.'

'One thing's for sure,' said Royce. 'With Jamerson taking my side, I won't be asking for a jury trial.'

Malone smirked. 'Haven't you heard? Justice is blind.'

'But people aren't.'

'I wouldn't worry about it. When push comes to shove, nobody shoves harder than Yale.'

Over the next few days Royce grew increasingly irritable, tormented by his confinement. There were only two positive things he could say about being in the jail. No one was shooting at him, and the food was better than the grub he got at the bunkhouse, because they brought it over from Betsy's Café.

Royce wondered over and over why he hadn't heard anything from Jamerson. Didn't they have to talk about the facts of the case? How could Jamerson defend him otherwise?

The day before the trial, Deputy Hawthorne brought him a neatly folded shirt and handed it to him. At first Royce didn't recognize it as his own.

'Miss Mueller dropped it off for you,' said Hawthorne, giving him a look that said he didn't deserve such favors.

When Royce unfolded the shirt, he saw that not only had it been mended better than he thought it could be, but Darlene had also ironed it. He sat on his bunk and just stared at it. Never in his life had he ever worn an ironed shirt. It was almost beautiful. Why would she do that? For the first time in days he smiled.

The next morning Foley and his deputies led him in handcuffs to the Grange Hall, which for today's purposes served as a courthouse. Royce wore his newly pressed shirt. As soon as he got inside, he spotted Jamerson and Malone sitting to one side. Malone gave him an amused smile. Jamerson merely nodded.

There were about twenty people gathered to witness the proceedings — not exactly a crowd. Darlene sat among them, conspicuously not looking at him. Foley took off his handcuffs and pointed him over to sit with Jamerson.

'First time I ever stood trial,' said Royce in a low voice as he sat down. 'I hope the judge is honest.'

'I hope he's not,' muttered Jamerson.

Just then a skinny man in a city hat entered the hall and took a seat at the table up front, facing everyone else. He took off his hat and called out in a voice that was bigger than he was.

'Are we ready to begin?'

'Ready, your Honor,' said Foley.

'First let me tell you folks who I am. I'm Judge Horace Donovan. And seeing as how this is my first time in Jawbone, I'll tell you how I do things. I keep it simple: what's right and what's wrong, what's legal and what's not. Now where's the prisoner and what's the charge?'

'Stand up, Royce,' said Foley. 'This man's the prisoner, and he's charged with assaulting one of my deputies.'

'Assaulting a law officer's a serious offense,' said the judge. 'Of course, if it wasn't, I wouldn't be here.'

Royce sat back down as Tom Pratt was called to the witness stand, which was just a chair next to the judge's table.

The judge said, 'You swear to tell the truth, so help you God?'

'I do.'

'Then tell it.'

Pratt said, 'This man Royce attacked

me when I tried to take him to the marshal's office for questioning. I fought back, then Deputy Hawthorne joined in, and finally Marshal Foley came with a shotgun and broke up the fight, and we took Royce into custody.'

'That about it, Marshal?' asked the judge.

'That's how it happened.'

Jamerson stood up. 'Is the marshal testifying? If so, he needs to take the witness stand.'

'You serving as defense counsel for the accused?'

'I am. He works for me. I'm Yale Jamerson.'

The judge turned to Foley. 'You swear to tell the truth, so help you God?'

'I do,' said Foley.

'No need sitting down for this. Just tell me what you saw.'

'I saw my deputies fighting with Royce.'

Jamerson stepped forward. 'But you didn't see how the fight started, did you?'

Foley hesitated. 'Well . . . no, I didn't see the very start of it.'

Speaking to Jamerson, but pointing to Pratt, who was still in the chair, Judge Donovan said, 'You got any questions for this one?'

'Yes, your Honor. Mr Pratt, you're the one who started the fight, isn't that true?'

'No, it's not.'

'Are you sure?'

'He hit me first. I'm dead sure of that.'

Jamerson half smiled. 'All right. No more questions.'

The judge signaled Pratt to leave the stand with an impatient wave of his hand.

Foley said, 'Now I'd like to call my other deputy, Jake Hawthorne.'

Jake stood up and started forward.

'Before we go through all that,' said the judge, stopping him in his tracks, 'did you see how the fight started?'

Jake glanced at Foley, then back at the judge. 'I saw the fight, but they were already going at it by then.'

'Then sit back down,' said the judge. 'Marshal Foley, you got any more evidence? Any more witnesses?'

'I don't think I need any more, your Honor. You've got the word of Deputy Pratt.'

'OK, Mr Jamerson, it's your turn. Do you have a defense you want to offer on behalf of the accused?'

'I do. I have one witness I want to call. Miss Darlene Mueller.'

Royce swung his head toward Darlene, who stood up perfectly erect and marched to the witness stand looking straight ahead.

The judge gave her a quick glance up and down. 'Miss Mueller, you swear to tell the truth, so help you God?'

'I do.'

'Have a seat.'

Jamerson walked up directly in front of her and looked at her for a moment. She returned his gaze with ice in her eyes.

'Miss Mueller, the incident in

question occurred outside your shop, is that correct?'

'It is.'

'Did you see what happened?'

'I did.'

'You saw who threw the first punch?'

'Yes.'

'Tell us who that was.'

'It was Deputy Pratt.'

'But Deputy Pratt testified the accused hit him first. So which is correct?'

'I suppose both are. Royce, that is, the accused, struck the first blow. But Deputy Pratt threw the first punch. He just didn't hit anything with it.'

A murmur of laughter rose from the spectators.

Jamerson smiled, too. 'What you're saying is, Pratt threw the first punch, but missed, then Royce defended himself by striking back.'

'That's how it happened.'

'Thank you, Miss Mueller.' Jamerson turned back to his seat.

Marshal Foley came forward. 'How is

it, Miss Mueller, that you just happened to witness something that took place out in the street?'

'I saw it through the window of my shop. Royce had just left.'

'Oh, I see. Royce is a friend of yours.'

'No, he's not. He was a customer. I sewed a shirt for him, and he had just walked out with it.'

'You've sewn more than one of his shirts for him, haven't you, Miss Mueller?'

She ignored his insinuation. 'I've sewn two. I make my living sewing.'

'And when a customer leaves your shop, do you make a habit of watching them as they walk away?'

'I have no such habit.'

'And yet, apparently, you were interested enough in the accused to be watching him when the fight started with my deputy.'

Darlene's cheeks reddened. 'I had no other customers at the time, and the fight took place directly outside my window. I heard your deputy order

Royce to come with him. I paid attention to what was going on. That's all.'

'So you heard Deputy Pratt order Royce to come with him. Then you must've heard Royce refuse to obey the command of a duly authorized officer of the law. And that's what started the fight, isn't it?'

'Pratt threw a punch. That's what started the fight.'

'He threw a punch in the performance of his duty. Isn't that the case here?'

'I have no idea what his duties are, or how he's expected to perform them.'

'You don't have much regard for the law, do you?'

'You're wrong. I do have regard for the law.'

'But you have more regard for the accused.'

Darlene bristled, but before she could say anything, Jamerson stood up.

'That's enough of that,' he said. 'We've heard the testimony we need to hear — everything that's pertinent.'

Judge Donovan chuckled. 'Yes, no sense hearing the impertinent testimony.'

The judge glanced around to see if anyone appreciated his little joke, but no one did, so he waved Darlene from the stand. Again she walked right past Royce as if he weren't there.

'Mr Jamerson, does your client wish to take the stand in his own defense?'

Jamerson turned to Royce with a questioning look. Royce stood up, but didn't move from his place.

'No, sir,' he said. 'Miss Mueller said it straight, and I'm satisfied with that.' Then he sat back down.

'Very well. Marshal Foley, Mr Jamerson — any closing arguments, gentlemen?'

Foley said, 'I've got a few. Mainly that a law officer has the right to use force when necessary. And when somebody fights against the law, he's breaking the law. Royce is guilty. Simple as that.'

'Mr Jamerson?'

'What's simple,' said Jamerson, 'is a man has a right to fight back when somebody takes a poke at him, even if that somebody's wearing a badge. It was clearly self-defense, so Royce isn't guilty of anything, other than being better in a fight.'

The judge looked around. 'OK, is that it? Everybody done? Here's my ruling. There's truth on both sides here. Royce was defending himself, plain enough. But the law's the law, and nobody can go around defying the law. So Royce is guilty. But he's not all that guilty. He deserves some jail time. And I figure what he deserves is about five days' incarceration.'

Foley grunted, and his deputies exchanged disgusted glances. Jamerson spoke up.

'Your Honor, Royce has already served five days.'

'That right? In that case, the defendant is free to go.'

Foley stood up. 'I think he oughta be

locked up for a lot longer than that.'

'You do?' said Judge Donovan. 'Then get yourself appointed circuit judge and you can do your own sentencing.' And with that he banged his gavel, put on his hat, and walked out of the Grange Hall.

Foley and his deputies soon followed, scowling their way past Jamerson and Royce.

'Justice,' said Malone, grinning. 'It's wonderful.'

The small crowd exited quickly, with Darlene first among them. Royce looked around the emptying hall, still a little dazed by the way things had gone.

Jamerson said, 'You look surprised to be a free man.'

'I'm surprised by a lot of things. How fast it all went. How easy the judge was on me. And most of all, that Darlene testified for me.'

'Why shouldn't she? She witnessed the whole thing.'

What really mystified Royce was Jamerson's relationship with Darlene.

When the two of them looked at each other just before she started her testimony, he could tell something was going on: defiance on her part; something else on his. It just didn't make sense. But making sense of it would have to wait for another day.

When Royce went to pick up his horse at the livery stable, he saw Judge Donovan riding out of town. Axel greeted him as he walked in.

'You're out of jail!'

'Thanks to the judge. I saw him leaving town just now.'

'And I can't figure it. He rode in late yesterday on a broken-down old nag, and today he rides out on a fine new horse.'

'He bought it?'

'Not from Pa. I don't know where he got it.'

Suddenly Royce had a fairly good notion about that.

When he got back to the ranch and went up to the house, Mrs Jamerson opened the door as usual.

'Hello, Royce. I'm glad to see you've been released.'

'Thank you. I'm pretty glad of it myself.'

'I understand Darlene Mueller testified for you.'

She said it casually, matter-of-factly, yet it made Royce pause briefly before he answered.

'Yes, she did.'

'That was nice of her.'

'Yes.'

'Yale is in his study. You may join him there.'

As Royce entered, Jamerson said, 'You ready to get back to work?'

'Good and ready, now that I'm free again. The way you handled things in court, you must keep some law books in here among all these others.'

'I do, not that I've read them very much. No, what mattered today was having a judge who saw things our way.'

'You might say he had a lot of horse sense.'

Jamerson looked sharply at Royce,

then burst out laughing. 'Yes. Horse sense. He had that, all right.'

'While he was still in town, why didn't you have him solve your other legal problems for you? About the tolls and the water rights.'

'Donovan's a criminal court judge. He doesn't handle civil disputes. Though I expect our civil disputes are going to turn very uncivil soon enough.'

'You mean with Foley.'

'He's holding back for some reason, and I don't know why.'

'What do you want me to do?'

'Spend more time in town. You and Malone. I have a feeling they're not going to strike the toll gates again, not just yet. Whatever's brewing, it'll show itself first in Jawbone. I'm pretty sure of that.'

'All right, then.'

'Just stay out of trouble. I don't want you ending up in jail again.'

'Me, either. Next time I might not have Darlene Mueller there to come to my defense.'

'I wouldn't recommend getting too involved with her,' said Jamerson.

'Any particular reason?' Royce hoped he would let something slip.

'When the town comes against us, she won't be on our side. In addition to that, a man like you and a woman like her just don't make a match.'

A man like me, thought Royce. He could take offense at that, and the expression on his face showed that he did.

'That wasn't an insult, Royce. It was just a statement of fact. You know it as well as I do. And I'm sure she knows it, too.'

'That's an awful lot of knowing. Seems to me the knowing doesn't come till after the learning.'

'I don't take you for a slow learner. Just remember what I said.'

10

Royce would've preferred staying out of Jawbone for a while, considering his enforced visit there for nearly a week, but following Jamerson's instructions, he and Malone rode into town the next day. At least this would give him a chance to see Darlene, no matter what Jamerson thought of it.

'I never paid Miss Mueller for fixing my shirt,' said Royce. 'I'll think I'll go take care of that.'

Malone gave him a sly grin. 'Always important for a man to pay his debts. Meet you later at The Last Apache.'

Royce rode a block over to Darlene's shop and was pleased to find her alone. She looked up when the door opened, but quickly looked down, then took a breath and looked up again.

'You don't seem all that happy to see me,' said Royce. 'You might not be seeing me at all if you hadn't testified for me yesterday.'

'I didn't testify for you. I testified for the truth.'

'A good thing for me the truth was on my side.' He pulled some money from his pocket. 'How much do I owe you?'

Her eyes flashed. 'I don't take money for telling the truth in court.'

'I meant for the shirt.'

'Oh.' She was momentarily flustered. 'A dollar will do it.'

'Last time it was fifty cents.'

'Last time it wasn't torn as much, or as bloody.'

'I do appreciate the washing.' He handed over the dollar. 'And the ironing.'

They both knew the ironing was more than was called for, and Darlene refused to meet his eyes. He waited for her to say something, but she didn't.

'Before the trial, I take it Jamerson came around looking for witnesses.'

'Yale Jamerson doesn't come in here.'

'Then you must've gone to him.'

This time she looked directly at him. 'Yes.'

'I heard he spent the night before the trial here in town, in his room above The Last Apache.'

'Did he?'

'Is that where you saw him?'

For a second he thought she might explode at him, but then something softer swept over her face.

'I wouldn't want you to have the wrong impression about my relation-ship with Yale. And you do have the wrong impression.'

'What's the right impression?'

'I don't talk about Yale, and Yale doesn't talk about me. That's all I care to tell you.'

An awkward moment stretched into several. Finally Royce said, 'Any more luck on getting that church built?'

'Not until we find a reliable source of lumber. You wouldn't be able to help with that, would you?'

'Me? I don't grow trees or cut them

down. Or carry them in wagons. Or pay the tolls for the freight.'

'Everybody pays a toll for what they do, one way or another,' she said.

'Reckon that's so.'

And with that note of agreement on something he didn't really understand, he took his leave, feeling dissatisfied in more ways than one.

Next he went over to the General Mercantile, where Mr Winston told him Jamerson's shipment of barbed wire had finally come in — from the south road, of course. There were six big spools of wire ready to be picked up, but since Royce didn't have a wagon with him, he told Winston he'd come back for it another day.

Heading out the door, he nearly bumped into Jake Hawthorne, who stopped to give him a contemptuous stare.

'You got a break from the judge, Royce. Don't count on it happening again.'

'I didn't count on it the first time.'

'If you were smart, you'd ride out of Jawbone and keep on going.'

Royce smiled. 'I can't even count the number of times I've been told that, in other towns and places. Not that I don't always appreciate the advice.'

'Here's a warning and no advice. When you ride outside the law, it's not always the law that brings you down.'

'Would you like to tell me what that means?'

'It means we don't need to waste our time dealing with the likes of you and Malone,' said Hawthorne. 'Let wolves fight wolves. That's all I've got to say.'

Hawthorne walked away, leaving Royce to wonder what wolves had to do with the happenings here in Jawbone.

He stopped by the livery stable to speak with Ludie Lundstrom, and afterward Doc Haney's office, and finally Betsy's Café. Pleasantries were passed at each location, but he learned nothing of any significance.

Later he joined Malone at The Last Apache, once again finding him in a card game with two other players.

'Winning?' said Royce.

'Not much. Not losing much, either.'

Footsteps coming down the stairs at the back of the room made Royce turn to look. First he saw the legs, a woman's legs, in stockings. Next he saw a frilly dress, then a shapely figure, a low-cut bodice, and last of all a pretty face — hard and cynical, but pretty. At the bottom of the stairs she stopped and scanned the room, looking every-one over. Her eyes held briefly on Royce, then kept on moving. When she had taken it all in, she walked casually down the length of the saloon until she reached the open door, where she stood looking out, either to see what she could see, or more likely to let herself be seen.

Royce sat at Malone's table just as the other men gave up the game on a losing hand. Malone smiled as he raked in all of four dollars. The two men edged past the woman at the door, giving her close looks as they passed.

She returned their looks with a direct stare that held no modesty or coy pretense.

'Who is she?' asked Royce.

'Ada Sayers. Been in town a few days. Miles rented her a room.'

Royce glanced over at Miles where he sat on a stool behind the bar, reading a penny dreadful with a lurid drawing on the cover of two men blazing away at each other while a woman cowered between them on the floor.

'I wonder if Jamerson knows how Miles is expanding his business.'

'He knows. Doesn't care.'

'Maybe Mrs Jamerson would care.'

'You gonna tell her?'

Royce shook his head. 'Hard to figure them out. Their relationship, I mean.'

'What's hard about it?'

'You think he's faithful to her?'

'Does it matter?'

'It would matter to her.'

Malone gave him a puzzled look. 'Maybe I should start calling you Preacher.'

'It's not a case of preaching. Just wondering why people do the things they do.'

'Most of the time it's not all that hard to figure. Just ask Ada.'

At the sound of her name she turned and said, 'What about Ada?'

Malone took a silver dollar, set it on edge in the center of the table and gave it a spin. Ada walked over and watched the spinning dollar as it slowed.

'What's that? An ante?'

'You feel like playing?'

She sat down and picked up the coin before it stopped. 'For a dollar?'

Malone pushed forward another four dollars.

She allowed the first glint of a smile Royce had seen from her. 'And what do I have to put up?'

'You know what,' said Malone, shuffling the cards. 'One hand of draw poker.'

Her eyes shifted to Royce. 'Let him deal.'

Malone looked mock offended. 'You

don't trust me?'

She repeated, 'Let him deal.'

Malone shoved the deck over to Royce, who shuffled it one more time and set it down close to Ada.

'Cut the deck,' he said.

She did, and he dealt out five cards to each of them.

'I'll take two cards,' she said, discarding two.

'And I'll take three,' said Malone.

Royce finished dealing and sat back to watch. Malone and Ada looked at their cards, then eyed each other silently for a moment.

Malone said, 'There's no raising or calling or folding. The bet's been made. Show me what you've got.'

'Two pair, jacks and fives,' she said, laying down her hand.

Malone held up his fanned out cards and turned them around. 'Three nines.'

Without a word and with only the smallest shake of her head to match an ironic half-smile, Ada got up and walked to the rear of the saloon and up the stairs. Malone stood up with a grin and pocketed his money.

'See you later.'

Then he followed her up the stairs.

Royce went over to the bar, and Miles looked up from his reading.

'Get you something?'

'Not right now. Except for some information. Ada. What's her story?'

Miles shrugged. 'Who knows? She rented a room. What she does with it is up to her.'

'Women and whiskey, guns and gambling. They turn saloons into powder kegs.'

'You're the one wearing a gun, not me. A friendly game of cards, a friendly drink, a friendly walk upstairs — nobody gets hurt by that.'

'You're wrong. Sooner or later, somebody always gets hurt.'

Later in the day, after several long and uneventful walks around town that took him into various places of business where he saw and overheard nothing of any consequence, he spotted Malone coming toward him along the street.

'Any news?' said Malone.

'No. Did you learn anything?'

'The only thing I learned was what a man can get with the help of three nines.'

'That's not what Jamerson will be wanting to hear.'

'As a matter of fact, I did hear something from Ada, who heard it from one of the deputies. Foley's bringing in some more help from out of town.'

'What does that mean?' said Royce. 'More trail tramps like those four we shot it out with at the gate?'

'Don't know. I'm guessing we'll find out soon enough.'

That evening Royce and Malone were back at The Last Apache, just about to leave for the ranch, when Sammy and George came in and joined them at the bar. After working the south toll gate all day, they were ready for a drink of something more than tepid water from a canteen.

'How was business?' asked Malone.

'Slow,' said Sammy. 'A wagon and a rider, about five hours apart.'

'They both turned back when they heard how much the toll was,' said George.

'Turned back cussing us and the Almighty and everything in between.'

'But no real trouble?' said Royce.

'Nobody got shot, if that's what you mean. How'd things go for you here in town?'

'Very quiet.'

With a sideways smile Malone said, 'I even stretched out for a little while this afternoon.'

That remark made Royce glance around at Ada, who was sitting between two men at the back table. Sammy and George looked that way, too, noticing her for the first time.

'Well, now,' said Sammy. 'Who's the good lookin' woman?'

Miles leaned forward from behind the bar.

'Name's Ada. Real nice gal. Maybe later you could buy her a drink.'

George said, 'Why don't we buy it for her now?'

Sammy bought a bottle from Miles, then together with George walked over to Ada's table.

'Hello, missy. Would you like to join us for a drink?'

She looked up. 'I would, but I'm busy right now.'

'That's right,' said one of the two men at the table. 'She's with us.'

'We can see that,' said George. 'But we think she'd be happier being with us.'

'Go drink your bottle someplace else,' said the other man.

Sammy said, 'We don't get to town that often, and it's been a long time since we had the chance to keep company with a lady.'

Ada snorted at the word 'lady.'

The two men with Ada exchanged looks. One said, 'You fellas with an outfit around here?'

'The YJ,' said George. 'Biggest outfit for five hundred miles.'

Again the two men passed silent thoughts before one spoke.

'Did you hear that, Drake? They work for the YJ.'

'We heard about the YJ,' said Drake. 'Kyle and me heard the YJ was nothing but a gang of thieves.'

'You heard wrong about that,' said Sammy.

'I don't think so,' said Drake. 'After all, here you are trying to steal our gal.'

'I'm nobody's gal,' said Ada.

'You're our gal for now,' said Kyle, who turned to George and Sammy. 'And we ain't giving her up. Sure not to a couple of YJ coyotes like you two.'

Sammy said, 'She's either gonna drink this bottle with us, or I'm gonna bust it over your head.'

At that the two men stood up, shoving their chairs back, and their hands hung by their guns. Sammy and George took a step or two backward, and Sammy switched the bottle to his left hand, leaving his right hand free to draw. Royce and Malone still watched from the bar; everyone else in the saloon was watching now, too. Ada sat stone still with only her eyes moving nervously.

'You lickspittle cowhands clear on out,' said Drake.

'You gonna make us?' said Sammy.

George glanced at Sammy with uncertainty and said in hardly a whisper, 'Sammy . . . '

'That's right,' said Kyle. 'We're gonna make you. Unless you show us that yellow streak down your backside as you scamper out the door.'

'That's not gonna happen,' said Sammy.

The four men stood in a frozen tableau for one second, two seconds, three seconds, four seconds, five seconds . . . then the tableau blew apart as four hands grabbed their guns and Ada screamed and two guns roared and Sammy's bottle broke on the floor. The whiskey spread and lapped against Sammy's body where it fell next to George's. Both men had their guns out of their holsters, but neither one had fired. They never had time.

Royce sensed Malone stiffen beside him. But just then Foley rushed through the saloon door with his gun out.

'What happened here?'

Drake and Kyle holstered their guns.

'Two men from the YJ called us out,' said Drake.

Foley looked to Miles. 'Who started it?'

'I guess I'd have to say it was Sammy and George.'

'Was it a fair fight?'

'It started fair,' said Miles, looking at the bodies. 'Didn't seem to finish that way.'

Ada was still quivering in her chair. She stood up unsteadily. Kyle reached out a hand to help her, but she jerked away from him, nearly falling down.

'You almost got me killed!' she said.

'Almost doesn't matter,' said Kyle, and Drake laughed.

Ada stormed away and headed up the

stairs. Foley turned to Royce and Malone and nodded over to the dead men on the floor.

'They were your men. You can take them back to Jamerson.' Then a strange little smile came on his face. 'This time you'll be carrying bodies back the other way.'

An hour later, in the darkness of the countryside as Royce and Malone rode along, each one leading a horse with a dead man slung across the saddle, Malone spoke aloud what Royce had been thinking.

'I don't believe the men who gunned Sammy and George just happened along.'

'No,' said Royce. 'They were too fast, and they pushed the fight too hard, though Sammy did his share.'

'They didn't seem all that riled up till George mentioned the YJ.'

'You know that help from out of town you heard Foley might be bringing in? I think it's already here.'

'Professionals. That's how I see it,

too. I wonder how much Foley is paying them.'

'Maybe Jamerson can buy them off,' said Royce.

'I hope not.'

Malone started to whistle softly as they continued riding toward the ranch. And there was something in that whistle more deadly and chilling than the cry of a coyote in the night.

Later Jamerson made it clear that he wasn't interested in buying anyone off.

'That's what I'm paying you two for,' he said.

'How do you want us to handle it?' said Royce.

'Any way you want to. But don't take chances with these men. They're gunfighters just like you.'

Just like us, repeated Royce in his mind. Just like us. The words gnawed at him, and he recalled what Hawthorne said: let wolves fight wolves.

11

The following day Royce went to the livery stable again to ask Ludie Lundstrom about the two gunmen.

'Are their horses still here?'

'They came and got them last night.'

'Any idea where they went?'

Lundstrom shook his head.

Axel had been listening and now spoke up. 'I know where they were headed when they first got in.'

'How would you know that?' said his father.

'Because they asked me.'

'Asked you what?' said Royce.

'Where they could find the marshal's office.'

Axel's information settled the whole thing in Royce's mind. There were no more doubts about who Kyle and Drake were working for.

Royce met up with Malone on the

street and told him what he'd found out.

'Where besides The Last Apache can a man rent a room in Jawbone?'

'No place else,' said Malone, 'unless they're staying with someone.'

So they walked into The Last Apache together, ready for whatever they might find, but at that time of the morning they found it empty. Only Miles was there, sitting at one of the tables, still reading the same dime novel.

'Haven't you finished with that thing yet?' said Malone.

'I'm reading it again,' said Miles. 'Not much else to do.'

'What you can do,' said Royce, 'is tell us which room those two gun hands are in.'

'They're not staying here. I only got four rooms, and they're all taken.'

Royce turned to Malone. 'Maybe we should ask your friend Ada. She was with them last night.'

Miles said, 'She's in room number — '

'I know what room she's in,' said Malone, heading for the stairs with Royce following.

Malone knocked on the door and waited. He knocked again.

'Who is it?' demanded Ada from inside. 'What do you want?'

'I want in.'

'Go away. It's too early.' Her voice was groggy, impatient.

Malone tried the door handle, then put his shoulder to the door and forced it open.

'Hey!' she yelled.

She was sitting up in a chair by the window, wearing a loose robe that didn't conceal very much. Beside her on the windowsill was a bottle, nearly empty. She made half an effort to pull the robe a little tighter, then looked around and found the bottle.

'Sorry I don't have any glasses.'

'We didn't come here to drink,' said Malone.

She smirked. 'No, I guess not.'

Royce said, 'We're looking for the

two men you were with last night
— Drake and Kyle.'

She took a drink from the bottle and
shrugged. 'You wanna look under the
bed?'

'Don't get smart,' said Malone.

'If getting smart was something I
could do, I wouldn't have ended up
here.'

'You talked to them,' said Royce.
'Did they tell you anything? Like where
they're staying?'

Her eyes began to focus better now
as she paid more attention. 'You're
gunning for them.'

'Never mind that,' said Malone. 'Tell
us what you know.'

'What I know,' she said bitterly, more
to herself than to them. 'And if I tell
you, what do I get out of it?'

Malone grabbed her arm. 'You get
out of it with no bruises.'

'Give her a chance to talk,' said
Royce.

'Yeah, give me a chance!' She jerked
her arm away. 'Men are always grabbing

me ... handling me ... pulling at me ... '

'We don't have time for your life's story,' said Malone.

'All right! They said they were staying at some farmhouse ... someplace south of here. They said the people who lived there had moved out.'

'The Hartwell place.'

'Yeah, that sounds like it.'

'You know it?' said Royce.

'Hartwell was a farmer who couldn't make a go of it, not after Yale cut back on the water. He and his family pulled up stakes a couple months ago.'

'Nice of someone to tip off Kyle and Drake where to find an out-of-the-way place to stay.'

'Someone nice who wears a star.'

An hour later they were riding up to the Hartwell farm. Barren fields surrounded what appeared to be an abandoned house, small but sturdy looking. A barn that wasn't much bigger stood away from the house. Royce and Malone pulled up and looked the place over from a distance.

'The smart thing to do,' said Malone, 'would be to hang back with rifles and pick them off when they come out.' He grinned. 'But what fun would that be?'

'I wonder if they're even in there.'

'No use wondering. Let's find out.'

They nudged their horses forward. It was all open ground between them and the house. No fences, no trees, no cover of any kind. Royce watched the windows for any sudden movement.

'Chimney,' said Malone.

A wisp of smoke drifted out of the chimney and dissipated in the steady breeze.

'They're in there, all right,' said Royce.

'And making themselves at home.'

'Their horses must be in the barn.'

Slowly they rode closer and closer until they finally stopped thirty yards from the door.

Malone said, 'If you'd like to go up there and knock, I'll watch your back.'

Royce gave him a look. 'Might as well be direct about it.' Then he called out,

'Hello the house!'

Several seconds passed, and they tensed for what would happen next. The door opened. Drake stepped out and over to one side, followed by Kyle, who stayed in the door.

'We weren't expecting visitors,' said Drake.

'We heard you had just moved in,' said Malone, 'so we came to pay you a little housewarming visit.'

'Mighty thoughtful of you,' said Kyle.

Drake said, 'You were both in the saloon.'

'When you gunned down Sammy and George,' said Royce.

'Is that who they were?' said Kyle. 'Being new in these parts, we didn't know one YJ rider from another.'

'You two must be Royce and Malone,' said Drake. 'If we had known that last night, your friends might still be alive. Of course, you wouldn't be.'

'Just so you'll know, this is Royce, and I'm Malone.'

'And we all know what this is about,'

said Royce. 'You came to Jawbone to gun us. So here we are.'

Drake smiled. 'You like to get right down to business, don't you?'

Malone said, 'I'm not as hasty as he is. I don't mind talking to a man before I kill him.'

'You must be pretty good,' said Kyle, 'to think it'll be that easy.'

Drake said, 'We're pretty good, too, as you saw last night.'

'The fact of the matter,' said Royce, 'is all four of us are good or we wouldn't all still be alive. And another fact of the matter is that when this is over, some of us won't be alive any longer.'

'Well, that's a pretty dreary way to look at it,' said Malone.

Kyle laughed. 'But he's right. We've all made our living the same way, and we'll do our dying the same way.'

'No need to rush it, though,' said Drake. 'We were just cooking up something to eat. Why don't you sit down with us?'

'A last meal?' said Royce.

'Professional courtesy,' said Malone. 'That's what it is, Royce.'

Royce just shook his head at this unexpected turn of events.

'Come on in,' said Drake.

The inside of the house felt cramped, though it only contained a wooden table with two straight chairs, a stool, and a small barrel to sit on. A dented iron kettle hung above the low flames in the fireplace.

'The people who lived here left a few things behind,' said Kyle. 'This kettle was one of them.'

'What's in it?' asked Malone.

Drake said, 'Prairie dog stew.'

'Been a long time since I ate a prairie dog,' said Royce. 'Or wanted to.'

Drake scrounged up some bowls from somewhere, and the four men sat down together, everyone's hands above the table. They ladled out the stew from the kettle sitting now in the center of the table. The prairie dog meat was chewy, but not distasteful. The men kept their eyes on each other as they ate, but their conversation became easier every minute.

'You fellas always ride together?' asked Royce.

'About a year now,' said Kyle. 'We teamed up in Abilene.'

'Texas or Kansas?'

'Texas. Our boss got tired of trail herds cutting across his land, so we spent some time making sure they didn't.'

Drake said, 'We worked that job till an angry trail boss shot the man we worked for.'

'I spent some time down in Texas myself,' said Malone. 'New Mexico, too. Lots of work in New Mexico.'

'How about you, Royce?' said Kyle.

'Those places, and others. Colorado for a while. Doing what we do doesn't keep us in one spot very long. Except for Malone's job here with Jamerson.'

'Good man to work for?' asked Drake.

'Good enough,' said Malone. 'Why?

Thinking of hiring on?'

Drake smiled. 'We already have a job.'

Royce said, 'Must be strange, working for a marshal.'

'Nobody's said we're working for him,' said Kyle.

'Foley sent for you to get us out of the way so he'd have an easier time with Jamerson.'

'Guess there's no use denying it,' said Drake. 'After all, pretty soon it won't matter to you, 'cause you'll be dead.'

'Or you will be,' said Malone.

'Then it won't matter to us, either,' said Kyle.

'Anybody else working for Foley?' asked Royce.

'Not that we've heard,' said Drake. 'I guess he figured we'd be up to the job.'

'At least you did a good job with the prairie dog,' said Malone, reaching into the kettle for some more stew.

They continued their meal, talking of places they had been and men they had worked for and dangers they had faced.

But underneath it all was the awareness that today would be the end for at least two of them.

'No use putting it off any longer,' said Drake at last.

'Outside?' said Malone.

They rose and settled their gun belts on their hips, put on their hats and walked out the door. Royce and Malone went to the left, while Drake and Kyle went to the right. Then they turned and faced each other, about fifteen feet apart.

Kyle said, 'I know a way we can do this.'

'I didn't know there was more than one,' said Royce.

'Do you hear that crow?'

'What crow?' said Malone.

They listened. Pretty soon they heard the caw of a crow from somewhere beyond the house, then silence again.

'I've been listening to him sound off ever since we got here,' said Kyle.

'And he's been threatening to shoot him,' said Drake.

'I might still do it,' said Kyle. 'But right now, the next time he sounds, that's when we draw.'

'Fair enough,' said Malone.

They stood there waiting, anticipating. Royce stood opposite Drake, while Malone faced Kyle. Three faces were set in stern concentration. Malone had a slight smile on his lips. Seconds ticked on . . . ten . . . fifteen . . . twenty . . . thirty . . . forty. When was that damn bird going to speak?

Caw!

The crow hadn't finished sounding before every gun flew out of its holster and four shots exploded in near unison. Three men fell. Malone fired quickly two more times, one each into Kyle and Drake, who both looked dead already, but he wanted to make sure. Then he turned to Royce, who sat up clutching his left shoulder. A dark stain was spreading on his shirt from underneath.

'How bad?' said Malone.

'Bad. You hit?'

'I think he took a mole off my neck.'

Royce snorted. He sure didn't feel like laughing. Malone helped him up on his horse. He slumped forward, hunching over to fight the pain and trying to keep the blood inside where it was supposed to be.

Malone started to mount up, then said, 'Just a minute.'

He went over and dragged the bodies of Kyle and Drake into the house, closed the door, then got back on his horse.

'So the buzzards won't get them,' he said.

'Get me to Doc Haney,' said Royce in a raspy voice, pressing a folded handkerchief to his wound.

Malone took Royce's reins and headed back toward Jawbone. Royce held on to the saddle horn with both hands, determined not to fall, and grimaced with the jostle of riding as a fog settled over his mind, broken only by the pain.

Malone glanced at him and said, 'You better not die on me.'

By then Royce was so disconnected from the world around him that he wasn't really sure he heard what Malone said next in a quieter voice.

'You're the only friend I've found worth having.'

When at last they came to Jawbone, Malone circled around to reach Doc Haney's house from behind. Royce tried to dismount slowly by himself, but suddenly Malone was there to catch him as he fell. He helped him inside without bothering to knock.

'Hey, Doc! You got a patient!'

Haney appeared, took one look and said, 'Bring him in here.'

In a moment Royce found himself on the operating table with Haney cutting away his shirt.

'I could've had that shirt mended,' said Royce.

'The hole was too big,' said Haney. 'No sense taxing Darlene's skill as a seamstress.'

'I guess that means the hole's pretty big in me, too.'

Haney looked at the wound with a dispassionate eye. 'This time I'd highly recommend the chloroform.'

'This time I'll take it.'

'Good,' said Malone. 'That means I won't have to hold you down and listen to you holler.'

'Should I even ask what happened?' said Haney, quickly assembling his surgical instruments.

Malone said, 'We had a nice little meal of prairie dog stew.'

'Lucky I didn't get shot in the stomach,' said Royce.

'I'll assume the prairie dogs didn't shoot you and let it go at that,' said Haney. He pressed a large wad of cotton over Royce's nose and mouth and began dripping chloroform on it. 'Breathe deeply and don't talk any more.'

Royce did as he was told, and moments later the room and the two faces looking down at him disappeared.

12

When Royce opened his eyes again, he saw a different room and different faces. He struggled to remember where he was and how he got there.

'Lie still.'

It was a woman's voice and a woman's face.

'Darlene,' he said, trying to sit up.

'I told you to lie still.'

'You better listen to her. You've been hurt pretty bad.'

Royce's blurry vision cleared and he recognized her brother Dan.

'Am I still at Doc's place?'

'No,' said Dan. 'You're at our house.'

'Just for a little while,' said Darlene quickly. 'Doc Haney didn't think you could stand the ride back to the ranch, even in a wagon.'

He was able to take a better look around him now and saw he was in a small bedroom with plain furniture. It wasn't a woman's room.

'Your room, Dan?'

'Yours for now. I'm bunking on the sofa.'

Royce raised a hand to feel the thick bandage on his shoulder. 'What did Doc say?'

'He said you owe him ten dollars,' said Darlene. 'And you'll be OK with rest. At least until you get shot again.'

'Darlene added that last part,' said Dan.

'I'm grateful to both of you for taking me in.'

'It wasn't our idea,' she said. 'I think Doc just didn't want to lose a regular source of income.'

'If he hadn't destroyed that shirt I was wearing, you'd be profiting, too.'

'So everybody profits from all this shooting, is that it?'

Dan started edging toward the door. 'I better get back to the store.' And he slipped away.

Royce pulled himself up a little more

in bed so he wouldn't be lying flat. He needed some elevation if he was going to tangle with Darlene.

'Nobody profits,' he told her.

'Certainly not the men you shot.'

'They were professionals. Foley brought them in.'

That information seemed to give her pause, but not for long.

'You make it sound as if that justifies the killing. But what if they had killed *you*?'

'What if they had?'

'Would that have been all right, too?'

'It would've been all right with them,' said Royce. 'How 'bout you?'

'What do you mean?'

'Would it have mattered to you?'

She hesitated. 'I feel sorry even when I see a rabid dog get shot.'

'That's the second time you've compared me to a dog.'

'That's not what ⸺' She shook her head in exasperation. 'Oh, get some sleep.'

'But I just woke up.'

'Doc left some extra bandages. Too bad he didn't leave some of that chloroform.'

She turned and stalked out of the room. And despite the pain in his shoulder, Royce smiled.

He stayed at the Winston house for nearly two weeks. During that time Darlene came in to check on him often, making sure his wound hadn't opened up again and sitting with him as he got better. Their relationship grew more comfortable and less confrontational. And yet there was always a sense of restraint on both their parts. For him, there was Darlene's unspoken, undefined relationship with Jamerson. And for her, there was the fact that he was one of Jamerson's hired guns.

As Royce recovered his strength, he spent many hours in the company of the Winstons, eating at their table, sharing their conversation, and learning more about the town and what it had suffered under the arbitrary control of one man, Yale Jamerson. Royce knew

Jamerson was slowly strangling the town, but he hadn't realized how bad things had gotten or how desperate the people had become.

After supper one night, Arthur Winston lit a pipe and summed it all up.

'That Jamerson, he's not a good man.'

Royce glanced at Darlene, but her face revealed nothing as her fingers kept sewing a blouse she'd brought home from the shop.

'Marshal Foley will take care of him,' said Dan.

'I'd like to know when,' said his father.

Royce said, 'I'd like to know that myself.'

This time Darlene's face showed some emotion, though it was hard for Royce to tell just what it was. She stopped her sewing.

'If the marshal 'takes care' of Yale Jamerson,' she said, 'he'll have to take care of you, too. And Malone.'

'Worried about Malone?' said Royce.

Dan laughed, and Darlene shot him a look before turning back to Royce.

'No,' she said. 'I'm worried about you.'

Her answer was so direct that he didn't know what to say.

'Thank you,' he said, and it sounded completely inadequate for what he was feeling. No one had cared what happened to him for many, many years.

Winston said, 'You should quit him.'

'Probably so.'

'Will you?' said Darlene.

'No. Not yet.'

Winston slowly puffed on his pipe. 'I've still got that load of wire.'

'I'll see that it gets picked up. I'll be going back tomorrow.'

'Tomorrow?' said Darlene with surprise and a little something else in her voice. 'Are you able?'

'Thanks to all the good care you've given me.'

'You can stay if you like,' said Winston.

'You've all been very kind. But I have work waiting for me.'

'Work,' said Darlene with distaste.

'Sure. I have to pick up that wire, don't I?'

The three men smiled. Darlene looked down and applied herself once more to her sewing, weaving the needle in and out along the blouse with a renewed and inexplicable intensity.

The next morning Royce eased on to his horse and rode to see Doc Haney, who examined the wound and changed the dressing.

'Either I'm a really good doctor or you're a really good healer. I suspect it's a bit of both.'

'It looks OK, then?'

'Well, it looks OK for a gunshot wound.'

'I can't settle the whole bill today, but I can give you five dollars now and the rest on payday.'

'Assuming you live till then,' said Haney. 'How much longer can you go on doing this, Royce?'

'What? Getting shot?'

'Somebody will kill you one of these days.'

Royce's smile faded away. 'I reckon they will.'

'That doesn't trouble you?'

'The value a man puts on his life depends on what sort of life he's got.'

'Or what sort of life he can hope to get. You're still a young man.'

'I don't feel that way. Haven't felt that way in a long, long time.'

Haney shook his head. 'I can't argue a man into changing the way he lives his life. He has to argue himself into that. I just hope you're still having that argument.'

Royce took his time riding back to the Jamerson ranch, and not just because of his still-tender wound. He was thinking about everything the doctor had said, and he thought about it all the way to the south gate, where he found Malone grinning up at him.

'You look good as new!' said Malone.

'Looks count for something, I guess.'

'That Miss Darlene must be a pretty good nurse.'

'She is.'

'Be sure to see Jamerson when you ride in. He's got something for you.'

'What is it?'

'Go see him and find out.'

Royce wasn't in the mood to go back and forth about it, so he rode on.

At the ranch house Mrs Jamerson ushered him inside, immediately solicitous about his condition.

'Yale and I have been quite concerned about you.'

'You and the Doc and Darlene. I'm not used to being so fussed over.'

Mrs Jamerson hesitated. 'I'm sure you were in good hands with Miss Mueller.'

He couldn't exactly tell how she meant that.

After being seated in the study, Royce took a series of long breaths as he waited for Jamerson, still unsure of what he was going to say to him. He'd let Jamerson talk first, and then

. . . well, it might be time to ride away.

Jamerson entered quickly and didn't give him a chance to talk first anyway.

'Royce, glad to have you back. I've got something for you.'

He reached inside a desk drawer for an envelope and handed it to him.

'What's this?'

'Open it up.'

Royce did, and at first glance it appeared to be his wages for the two weeks he'd been laid up. But looking closer, he saw it was at least four times his normal wages.

'Lot of money.'

'It's yours. I did the same for Malone. Actually not as much, since you got shot up and he didn't.'

'First time I got a bonus for being too slow.'

Jamerson laughed. 'You both did a good job getting rid of Drake and Kyle. It showed Foley those tactics won't work.'

'He could still bring in more men.'

'I don't think he will. Malone's heard

talk around town that folks weren't too happy with Foley for bringing in those gunmen. They expected Foley and his deputies to do all the dirty work. Their idea of civilizing the town didn't include using hired killers.'

Royce looked down at the money in his hand. 'Maybe they figured there were enough hired killers in town already.'

'The way I see it, it's Foley and his men who meet that description. And that makes the people in town nothing but hypocrites, not to mention cowards.'

'Where there are laws, there have to be lawmen. Hard to get around that.'

'But I have, and I will.'

Royce sat there thinking he should give the money back to Jamerson and simply go. But go where? And do what? He was good at doing one thing, and he had just earned extra for doing it well, or at least well enough to stay alive. He sighed in resignation and put the money in his pocket.

13

Royce took a wagon into town the next day to pick up the wire that Arthur Winston was holding for Jamerson. As he rode past the bank, he suddenly pulled up and smiled at what he was thinking. A minute later he walked into the bank and approached the teller's window.

'Good morning,' said the teller, neither friendly nor unfriendly.

'Morning,' said Royce.

That was when Zachary Phelps came out of his small office.

'What do you want?' he asked. 'Not here to rob us, are you? Jamerson's already bleeding this town dry.'

'I take it Mr Jamerson doesn't keep his money in your bank.'

'I asked you what you wanted.'

Royce pulled out the folded wad of extra pay that he had in his pocket and laid it down in front of the teller.

'I didn't come to take money out, Mr Phelps. I came to put some in.'

The look on Phelps' face was reward enough for tolerating his insults.

'You mean you want to open an account?'

'I don't like carrying around this much folding money. And I didn't want to leave it in the bunkhouse. You think it'll be safe in your bank?'

'Of course it'll be safe here. I just didn't think that you . . . that is . . . I didn't take you for the sort of man who would have a bank account.'

'If I get one now, I guess I will be.'

Phelps turned to the teller. 'Mr Beckworth, please open an account for this man.'

'Yes, sir, Mr Phelps.'

Then with a final confused look at Royce, Phelps went back into his office.

With his new account book in his pocket, Royce climbed up on the wagon and continued to the General Mercantile, where Arthur Winston was behind the counter and Dan was stocking shelves. They both looked surprised to see him.

'We didn't expect you back so soon,' said Winston. 'You should still be resting.'

'I've had my fill of resting. Today I came for that wire.'

Winston walked out from around the counter, favoring his bad leg as always.

'Dan, go get the wire and load it in the wagon for Royce.'

'Sure thing,' said Dan, heading into the back storeroom.

'I'll help him,' said Royce.

'Don't hurt that shoulder.'

'I won't.'

Royce followed Dan and found him trying to lift one of the spools of barbed wire.

'Hold on,' said Royce. 'You take one end, I'll take the other. Easier that way, and neither one of us gets cut up.'

Together they carried one spool at a time out to the wagon, with Royce using mainly his right arm to lessen the strain on his other shoulder. On their final trip to the storeroom for the last spool, he looked around at all the items cluttering the room. There were farm implements, boxes of jars, bolts of cloth, hammers and nails, and sundry other pieces of hardware.

'You're able to sell all this?' said Royce.

'I wish. Some of it we ordered to stock the store before folks slacked off buying. And some of it people had us order for them special, but when it came in, they couldn't pay for it.'

'Because of the town getting squeezed by Jamerson.'

'That's how it is.'

Royce caught sight of a sturdy wooden crate with lettering on the side, and it made him look twice.

'Dynamite? Who ordered dynamite?'

Dan hesitated for a second, as if unsure of whether he should answer.

'It was Foley.'

'Foley,' said Royce, wondering what use a marshal would have for dynamite.

'I'm guessing he's not going to use it to clear stumps.'

'He didn't say. But he hasn't come for it yet.'

Without saying anything more, they carried out the remaining spool of wire. The six spools filled up most of the wagon bed. Winston stepped outside to look.

'Got it all?'

'That's the last of it,' said Royce. 'Jamerson paid for it in advance, didn't he?'

'Yes, but what he paid me is already gone. We can't last much longer if things don't change.'

Royce didn't try to argue that. He said goodbye and drove on to the doctor's house, where he paid Doc Haney the other part of his fee. After that he came back through town to Darlene's shop.

She looked up and smiled hello as he came in — the first time she had ever smiled when he entered the shop.

'How are you?' she asked.

'Doc says I'm fine, so I'll go along with that.'

'What are you doing in town?'

He pointed to the wagon outside. 'I picked up some wire for Jamerson.'

'Hasn't he already fenced all there is to fence?'

'There's been a lot of downed wire lately, which is what happens when people cut it.'

'And cutting wire is what happens when somebody like Yale puts it up.'

'I didn't come in to talk about wire,' said Royce. 'Will you have lunch with me?'

'Lunch? I'd have to close the shop.'

'I'm the only customer you've got. And I'm buying.'

She smiled again then. 'I suppose I could get away for lunch.'

After locking up, they walked over to Betsy's Café. Royce steered Darlene toward a back table where they'd have a bit more privacy.

As lunch progressed, they fell into a relaxed conversation that hadn't been possible before his convalescence at the Winston house. Now that some of the barriers between them were down, a former question occurred to him.

'Darlene Mueller,' he said, musing over the name.

She raised her eyebrows. 'Yes?'

'Mueller was your mother's name, I understand.'

'That's right. Until she married Arthur Winston.'

'She became a Winston, but you didn't.'

'I was four years old at the time. A year later my mother died giving birth to Dan. Maybe I should've taken the name Winston, but I was a stubborn little girl — heartbroken little girl — who didn't want to forget her mother or cast away her name. So I kept it.'

'Which proves there's a simple explanation for everything.'

'Not everything,' she said, and then she turned the conversation to something else.

Royce walked Darlene back to the shop after lunch, then headed through town on the wagon. As he approached the jail, Deputy Hawthorne saw him coming and stepped inside. Then as Royce drew even with the jail, Marshal Foley came out and held up his hand. Hawthorne and Pratt followed behind him. Royce reined in.

'What is it, Marshal?'

'You going back to Jamerson now?'

'I am if you let me.'

'We'll do better than that,' said Foley. 'We'll give you an escort. After all, we wouldn't want you to run afoul of any road agents trying to steal this valuable wire.'

Foley and his deputies mounted their horses, and as Royce slapped his team of horses into motion again, Foley and Hawthorne rode along on either side of him while Pratt rode behind.

'I never thanked you, Marshal, for that free room and board you gave me,' said Royce.

'Maybe next time you can stay longer.'

'Care to tell me what you plan to do when we get to the ranch?'

'We plan to talk to Mr Jamerson.'

From the other side of the wagon Hawthorne said, 'Talk to him first, anyway.'

'I hope you're not going to offer him some of that free room and board.'

Foley said, 'In case you haven't noticed, the law has come to Jawbone.'

Royce made a show of looking behind him. 'And in case *you* haven't noticed, we just rode out of Jawbone.'

'The law is bigger than any one town,' said Foley. 'And that reminds me. We found a couple of men shot in a farmhouse a few miles from here. You wouldn't know anything about that, would you?'

'Maybe they shot each other.'

Foley's face said all there was to say.

They rode the rest of the way in silence until they approached the south gate of the ranch, where two hands named Barney and Justin were standing guard. That was when Foley spoke once more to Royce.

'If you try anything, one of the three of us will take you down. Pratt's right behind you and can pick you off.'

Then they were at the gate, and the guards looked inquiringly at Royce.

'It's OK. Let us through.'

Barney didn't look convinced. 'If you say so, Royce. But I don't know if Mr Jamerson's gonna like seeing these fellas.'

Hawthorne said, 'That's none of your business.'

'It could be, plenty fast,' said Justin.

'Don't be stupid, cowboy,' said Foley.

Royce said, 'Nobody's going to be stupid. Not yet.'

Barney opened the gate and stood back as they came through.

'They should've paid the toll, just the same,' said Justin in a loud voice.

'No charge today,' said Royce, looking at Foley. 'At least not coming in.'

As Royce and the lawmen passed, Barney and Justin closed the gate, exchanged glances, then mounted their horses and trailed behind them.

As they drew near the ranch house, Foley reached down and pulled a shotgun out of his rifle boot. Hawthorne and Pratt did the same.

Royce said, 'That won't help you if you try to take Jamerson.'

'It'll help if Jamerson tries to take *us*,' said Foley.

Royce stopped the wagon at the house and jumped down. His knock on the door brought Mrs Jamerson. She looked past Royce at the marshal and his men, still on their horses.

'Is Mr Jamerson here?'

'No,' she said. 'He rode out with Malone two hours ago. Some of the men found twelve head of cattle that were shot during the night. Who would do a terrible thing like that?'

'Maybe we should report it to the marshal,' said Royce. He turned and said, 'This is Mrs Jamerson.'

'Ma'am,' said Foley, giving her a polite nod. 'If somebody's shooting Jamerson cattle, it's probably because that's the only way they know how to strike back.'

'Do you suppose you could find whoever did it?' she asked.

'Right now I'm just trying to find your husband.'

'He should be returning soon. You may come in and wait, if you wish.'

'Thank you, ma'am. We'll do that.'

Foley signaled to his men, and they dismounted, still carrying their shotguns.

'Royce, would you please join us?' she said.

He was surprised she asked, and he took it to mean she was concerned for Jamerson, though her outward manner was calm and gracious.

Barney and Justin, who had kept their distance, rode away quickly now, and Royce knew they were headed off to get Jamerson.

Inside, Mrs Jamerson led her guests

into a well furnished parlor. The men took off their hats as they settled uneasily on the sofa and upholstered chairs.

'Please make yourselves comfortable, while I bring some tea.'

Pratt and Hawthorne, together on the sofa, looked at each other with dubious anticipation of the idea of tea, but Foley thanked her as she left the room. He and Royce had seated themselves on straight-backed chairs, better suited to quick action if necessary. The lawmen held their shotguns in their laps, and Royce suspected they felt as awkward as they looked. He smiled.

'Something funny?' said Foley.

'The three of you. No, the four of us. But I don't think Mrs Jamerson is very amused by your visit here.'

'Jamerson stopped coming into town,' said Pratt. 'This was the only way to see him.'

'And what happens when you do?'

'That's up to him,' said Foley.

Soon Mrs Jamerson returned with a

tea service on a tray and set it on a low table. She then proceeded to pour the tea into five cups of good china. The men accepted the cups carefully from her hand and sat holding them as if they were uncertain what to do next. After serving everyone else, Mrs Jamerson sat down with her own cup of tea, then spoke to Foley in the most casual of voices.

'Have you come to kill my husband?'

'What? Why . . . no, ma'am,' said Foley, one hand holding a teacup and the other hand a shotgun.

'Arrest him, then?'

'We just want to talk to him.'

'I see. Do you like the tea?'

'Very good, ma'am.'

Pratt and Hawthorne mumbled the same.

Royce sipped his tea and said, 'Fine china is hard to come by out here. When Mr Jamerson gets back, you might want to remove it before all the talking starts.'

She nodded as if understanding his

suggestion. He smiled grimly at the lawmen and took another sip of tea.

Much talk about the weather followed, interspersed with even greater amounts of silence. Finally Royce spotted four riders through the window. Justin and Barney split away toward the south, while Jamerson and Malone continued on to the house.

'He's coming,' said Royce.

'I'll leave you gentlemen to discuss your business,' said Mrs Jamerson, collecting their cups and discreetly withdrawing from the room.

A minute later Jamerson and Malone entered. By then all the men were on their feet. Jamerson took note of the shotguns.

'I trust you didn't find my wife too dangerous.'

Foley ignored the comment. 'Jamerson, it's time to finish this.'

Malone eased around one side of the room, drawing glances from Pratt and Hawthorne.

'I agree,' said Jamerson. 'The only

question is how.'

'Open the road. Tear down the dam. If you don't, we will.'

'To do that, Marshal, you'd have to do an awful lot of killing.'

'I've done an awful lot of killing before.'

'Yourself?' said Malone. 'Or did other people do it for you?'

Foley gave him a contemptuous look. 'I won't be stopped by cheap gunmen.'

'Cheap?' said Malone in mock offense. 'You think we should ask for a raise?'

'The West is littered with the bones of men like you,' said Foley.

'And like you,' said Jamerson. 'And like me. What does that prove? Whenever you're ready for a showdown, Foley, I'll be happy to accommodate you.'

'Your wife asked me if I came here to arrest you. I'm telling you now, Jamerson, I *will* arrest you the next time you ride into Jawbone. I'm making you a prisoner on your own ranch. Come into Jawbone again and you'll end up in a cell — or a grave.'

'As you said, it's my ranch and now I'm ordering you and your men off it.'

Malone said, 'We could send them back to town all trussed up. Royce even brought the wire.'

A deadly, still moment hung in the air. Royce considered the three shotguns being held at the ready and hoped the moment would pass.

'They ride out,' said Jamerson. 'But don't ever come on my land again, Foley, because next time you won't leave.'

Foley gave him a hard stare, then turned to his men. 'Come on.'

They left the room and walked out of the house, got on their horses and rode away.

Royce had seen all this play out before in many different settings, but there was only one way it ever ended, and that was with bloodshed and men dying on the ground.

'I was wondering,' he said, 'what's to

be gained by all this.'

'What do you mean?' said Jamerson.

'What would it hurt to give the town back its water and lower the tolls?'

Malone said, 'Don't tell me you're on their side?'

'If I were on their side, I'd be riding with them. I'm just asking if it wouldn't be better to let the town survive. Then they'd call off Foley.'

'No,' said Jamerson. 'A small settlement and a handful of farmers, I didn't much mind. But if I don't stop them now, there'll be no stopping them at all. A few dozen people have already turned into a few hundred, and before long they'll turn into a few thousand, then thousands more. I can't fight thousands. But I can and will fight the few that come against me now. Are you still with me?'

'If I ever decide to pull out, you'll know it,' said Royce. 'Because I'll tell you.'

'Fair enough.'

What Royce didn't tell Jamerson was

what he suspected Foley was planning to do with the case of dynamite waiting for him in the back room of the General Mercantile. He told himself he couldn't be sure and it would be better to wait and see what happened. But deep down he had to admit that a part of him wanted his suspicion to be true and that he'd rather not do anything to stop it.

14

In the early dusk, hours after Foley and his deputies left, two cowhands who had ridden out to relieve Barney and Justin at the south gate came riding back in a hurry with grim news. They had found both men on the ground, killed by shotgun blasts, with the gate standing wide open. Pinned on Barney's shirt was a note: 'They resisted arrest.'

Jamerson looked down at the blood-stained note they handed him, then crumpled the note and threw it aside.

'If that's how they want it, that's how it'll be. We're going to Jawbone.'

'How many men?' said Malone.

'Just you, me, and Royce. Three against three.'

'When?' said Royce.

'Tonight. And we're taking shotguns.'

Royce didn't like the idea of going

right away when they'd likely be expected, or going at night, or fighting with shotguns at close quarters. All of those together increased their chances of getting killed. But Jamerson was determined to see it through, and Royce figured this would at least settle the matter quickly, one way or the other.

When Jamerson had calmed down he listened to Royce's advice that they wait and ride in around two or three in the morning, long after Foley would have given up on their coming that night. They could go up the back stairs to the room Jamerson kept at The Last Apache and wait there till dawn. Then they'd have a much better chance of surprising Foley and defending themselves in daylight from any ambush.

Hours later there was a slim crescent moon hanging over Jawbone when Royce, Malone, and Jamerson rode into view of the town. No lights were burning. They slowly circled the town, looking for any sign of Foley or his men. Then in single file they rode to the livery stable, put their horses in empty stalls, and closed the stable door behind them when they left.

Watching for any movement among the buildings as they made their way along, they came into the alley behind The Last Apache and went up the back staircase. Quietly they slipped into the upstairs hall and entered Jamerson's room.

'No lamp tonight,' whispered Jamerson. 'We'll wait in the dark.'

Royce settled into a chair by the window, while Malone sat in one next to the locked door. Jamerson reclined on the bed with his shotgun beside him.

'I can see the jail from here,' said Royce. It was farther down the street, almost out of his field of vision.

'Good,' said Jamerson. 'Let me know if anyone goes in or out.'

Malone said, 'You think they sleep in the jail?'

'Hawthorne and Pratt took turns in the other cell while I was there,' said

Royce. 'If I were them, that's where I'd be tonight.'

'We'll find out in the morning,' said Jamerson. 'These next few hours will go slow.'

'I know how I'd like to spend the next couple of hours,' said Malone. 'Ada's sleeping two doors down.'

'Just listen for anyone in the hall. And Royce, keep watching the street.'

There wasn't much else for them to do during the minutes and hours that followed. Most of their waiting time was taken up by long silences, broken only occasionally when they spoke in low, night-time voices.

When just the faintest glow showed itself on the eastern horizon, Royce saw a figure walking up the street. He peered into the gloom, trying to make out who it was. A woman. Betsy, heading toward her café to start the day.

'Anything?' said Jamerson, who had seen him lean forward.

'No.'

Malone stretched in his chair. 'Daylight's coming.'

'Foley and his deputies ought to be stirring soon,' said Jamerson.

'I never killed a lawman before,' said Malone, sounding unconcerned at the prospect. 'How about you, Royce?'

'No,' he said. 'I outran a few.'

'Running's one thing I have no intention of doing,' said Jamerson, sitting up on the side of the bed. 'I may get killed off, but I won't be run off.'

Suddenly Royce sat up straighter. 'A light just went on in the jail.'

'Can you tell who's there?' said Jamerson, joining him at the window.

'No.'

Malone was on his feet. 'Whatever we're going to do, we better do it, unless you figure on making them come up here.'

Royce nodded in agreement. 'We could wait a long time for all three of them to show up together. By then a lot of other people will be out on the street.'

'All right then, let's go,' said Jamerson, reaching over to the bed for his shotgun.

Malone unlocked the door quietly and stepped outside, followed closely by Royce and Jamerson. Suddenly a door opened a few feet down the hallway and Ada stepped out in her undergarments and a thin robe. She was looking back into the room the other way and didn't see them.

'No, no you've had enough,' she said. 'Go on, now.'

'You go on and get me some breakfast,' said a man's voice, and a second later Hawthorne stepped into the hall, wearing just his trousers. Instantly he whirled back into the room as Malone raised his shotgun and raced forward.

'What the hell!' said Ada, jumping back.

Malone reached the doorway, then ducked to the other side just before a shotgun blast from inside the room blew through the open door and ripped into Ada, who bounced back against the wall and fell. Malone pointed his shotgun around the doorway and fired blindly, then drew his gun and stepped inside, firing one-two-three shots. Royce and Jamerson looked into the room. Hawthorne lay dead on the floor; behind them, Ada groaned softly. Royce knelt beside her as she died.

'That should bring somebody!' said Jamerson. 'Royce, go down the back way. Malone, you come with me.'

As Jamerson and Malone headed down the stairs into the saloon, Royce hurried down the back staircase and into the alley. The gauzy light of dawn made the town visible now. Royce looked around the edge of the building toward the jail. The door was open; whoever had been inside wasn't there any longer. He heard the front door of The Last Apache open and saw Malone poke his head out carefully. Then Jamerson burst past him into the street, clutching his shotgun.

'Foley!' he yelled. 'Here I am! Back in

town! Come and arrest me!'

Royce and Malone edged out a step from their cover, looking in all directions. Royce still held a shotgun, but Malone had left his upstairs. Suddenly a voice rang out from somewhere down the street.

'I don't know who you were shooting at, Jamerson. But I'm going to put you and your gunfighters in jail or in the ground, soon as my deputies get here, and you can bet they'll be here soon.'

'One of them won't!' said Jamerson. 'And that makes up for one of the two men you murdered yesterday!'

At that word a shotgun blast from a distance stung Jamerson in the leg, dropping him to one knee. Malone rushed out and grabbed him and hauled him back into the saloon. Royce could tell now that Foley was farther away than he thought he'd be, somewhere beyond the General Mercantile. He turned and went the other way down the alley, circling to the street behind and making his way toward

Foley, watching all the time for Pratt to show up, too.

Everything was quiet again now, except for a dog barking somewhere, aroused by the gunfire. After going what he hoped was far enough, Royce cut back through another alley, thinking he was coming up on the other side of Foley's position, which he took to be on the opposite side of the street. Foley's shotgun hadn't served him very well against Jamerson from so far away, but Royce might be on top of him any minute now, so he held his own shotgun ready.

Nearing the corner, he suddenly heard footsteps. They were on his side of the street and coming closer, telling him he must've misjudged where Foley was hiding. He set himself with the shotgun pointed at the corner, but just when he expected Foley to come into sight, he heard him call out from somewhere across the street.

'Look out, Pratt! He's in the alley!'

Royce jumped back and flattened

himself against the side of the building, but Pratt didn't come around the corner blasting as Royce assumed he would. Instead, Pratt hesitated at the corner with the end of his shotgun extending into the open by about eight inches, just six feet away. Royce aimed and fired, blowing Pratt's shotgun out of his hands. Then he drew his Colt and rushed forward, veering to the other side of the alley. As soon as Pratt came into view, Royce saw him pulling his six-gun, so he didn't hesitate. He put two slugs into Pratt before he could get off a shot. And yet a bullet came whizzing by him, and then another: Foley was firing at him from inside the open door of the General Mercantile. He ducked into the alley again.

Royce figured his best chance was to do what he had set out to do originally, so he ran to the street behind him and this time went to the very end of town, just a few buildings farther down, then dashed across the street toward the General Mercantile, working his way along the fronts of the buildings as he moved closer and closer to Foley. He saw Malone heading his way from the other direction on the same side of the street. Royce signaled to him where Foley was making his stand.

The store had plate glass windows on both sides of the door. When Royce and Malone reached opposite edges of the store and stopped, Royce fired a shot through the big window beside him, shattering it, and Malone quickly did the same with the window on his side. They fired into the store several more times, then paused to listen. Royce heard movement toward the rear of the store.

'He's going out the back!'

Royce rushed around the side of the store and reached the corner just as Foley came out of the back storeroom. Foley saw him and threw a careless shot in his direction before dodging back into the store. Royce held up at the corner, waiting. A moment later an exchange of several shots broke the silence, and once again Foley burst through the door, only this time he was doubled over and his gun hung loosely at the end of his arm. He looked over at Royce, unable even to raise his gun to defend himself. Royce stood still, then another gunshot sounded from inside the store and Foley jerked and collapsed. Malone walked out to stand over him.

'That's the end of the law in Jawbone.'

'Looks that way,' said Royce, holstering his gun with a weary feeling.

'This should make Jamerson happy.'

'How bad was he wounded?'

'Not bad,' said Malone. 'He'll need some tending.'

'I'll get Doc Haney and bring him over.'

Royce found Haney standing on his porch, waiting, his medical bag at his feet.

'Anybody injured?' he asked. 'Or just dead?'

'Both. It's Jamerson.'

'Which one is he? Injured or dead?'

'Leg wound.'

For a second Haney looked disappointed, then he shrugged and picked up his bag.

'At least I know he can pay the bill.'

When they got to The Last Apache, Jamerson was sitting in a chair with his right pant leg torn open to his thigh, revealing several knicked-up patches of flesh.

'It's nothing,' he said as Haney knelt to examine his leg.

'It's a nothing that could turn into gangrene if it's not treated.'

'There may be some lead still in there,' said Jamerson.

'An excellent diagnosis. Fortunately for you, none of it went into the bone.'

Malone stood at the bar, having a free drink since Miles still hadn't shown himself. 'Want us to take him to your office, Doc?'

'I can do what I need to do right here, but not while he's in that chair.' He looked around. 'The table's too small. On the bar. I need you laid out on the bar.'

Jamerson smiled wryly. 'Somehow being 'laid out' doesn't sound too encouraging. I trust your procedure won't prove fatal.'

'Not as fatal as your procedure turned out for Foley and his deputies.'

'It was Foley who shot me. And he did it from hiding, like a coward. We were defending ourselves.'

'I'm not your judge, Mr Jamerson, but I do have the privilege of being the only man who can stick a knife in you without getting killed for it.'

Royce and Malone lifted Jamerson and set him on the bar, where he stretched out on his back with his right leg facing the doctor. Haney quickly discovered that most of the shot had merely torn the flesh while passing through. He had to remove just two pellets, and they weren't hard to get out.

'A good thing for you that Foley wasn't closer.'

'I wish he had been, so I could've gotten a shot at him.'

'Oh, you shot him, all right.' Haney glanced at Royce and Malone. 'By proxy.'

Malone acknowledged the credit with a smile as he leaned over to wipe the dust off his boots.

'In case you didn't know,' said Jamerson, grimacing at the doctor's probing, 'Foley gunned down two of my men yesterday and challenged me to come into town. He's the one who forced it.'

Haney finished treating the wounds and began bandaging Jamerson's leg. 'Anyone else in need of attention?'

'Not from you,' said Malone. 'But three ex-lawmen will keep the undertaker busy.'

'And the woman,' said Royce. 'Ada.'

'That's right,' said Malone. 'I nearly forgot about her.'

Haney looked at him coldly. 'You killed a woman?'

'Not me,' said Malone. 'Hawthorne

213

shot her. Accidentally.'

'Oh well, then. As long as it was accidental,' said Haney with his finest sarcasm. Then he turned to Jamerson: 'Congratulations on your success in reducing the population of Jawbone while expanding its cemetery. Keep on this way and it'll be a ghost town before long. But just remember, you'll be a ghost, too, someday.'

Jamerson sat up on the bar. 'Fine with me. A ghost doesn't have to listen to any preachy doctors. How much do I owe you?'

'Thirty dollars.'

'Thirty! That's a little steep, isn't it?'

'It was a house call. But if you'd rather I put those pellets back where I found them . . . '

Jamerson pulled out a wad of cash and handed over the thirty dollars. Haney stuffed the money in his pocket, closed his bag, and left the saloon. Royce followed him out. They both stopped on the small porch and silently surveyed the street.

A few people had ventured out, most of them gathering around Pratt's body, but not too close to it. They looked as if they had lost someone important to them, and of course they had, even though they had barely known him. They had lost what he and Foley and Hawthorne represented: a chance for progress and the rule of law.

'There's more death than life in this town now,' said Haney.

'Only the living can tell the difference,' said Royce. 'By the way, I notice you didn't offer Jamerson any chloroform when you went to work on him.'

'I figured he could stand the pain. I figured he deserved it.' He glanced at Royce. 'Physical pain is one thing. But can you chloroform a conscience? Maybe you've found a way.'

Royce didn't answer. He had no answer to give.

15

Jamerson decided to stay overnight in his room at The Last Apache. Miles reappeared and arranged for the undertaker to cart away the bodies of Hawthorne and Ada from upstairs. Then he cleaned out Ada's room so Royce could move in and stay close to Jamerson. Malone took the room between them, right next to Jamerson's, forcing out the drunk who had slept there through the entire shoot-out.

Miles was still scrubbing Ada's blood off the hallway floor and walls when Royce stood inside the room looking down at her few possessions, piled together in a small weathered trunk. There were two or three dresses and some other clothes, plus a jewelry box that held a few combs and cheap bracelets and necklaces, along with a yellowed photograph of a man and woman and a young girl. He recognized Ada as the girl.

Miles stood up from his chore and looked into the room.

'I got up all the deputy's blood, I think. Lucky you didn't shoot him on the bed.'

'Malone shot him.'

'Well, whoever shot him, he's just as dead,' said Miles. 'It'll be a while before I can patch up all the holes from the shotgun blast.'

'That's fine,' said Royce. 'Doesn't matter.'

'Don't know what I'm gonna do with Ada's stuff.'

Royce shut the trunk lid, closing out her life. 'Burn it or bury it, or maybe hang it over the bar next to the Apache scalp — another memorial to somebody who'll be remembered more for what she was than for who she was.'

Miles nodded dumbly, then went on downstairs with his bloody rags.

Royce wandered over to the General Mercantile, where he found Arthur

Winston examining all the damage to his store while Dan swept up the broken glass. Winston's unhappy face deepened its displeasure when he saw Royce.

'Look at this place! Broken windows, broken door, glass everywhere, bullets in the merchandise . . . '

'Foley broke the door to get in. He picked this spot, not us.'

'Foley, oh yes . . . Foley, who I found outside my back door, shot dead. Your work, I'm guessing.'

'No, it was Malone.' Royce observed wryly to himself that he kept getting credit for Malone's handiwork.

'Huh,' said Winston. 'Like it makes any difference.'

'I'm sorry about your store. I'll ask Jamerson to pay for the damages.'

'I don't want anything from Jamerson! He's killing this town, and there's nobody left to stop him.'

Royce knew anything he said would just inflame the shopkeeper more, so he left the store and went over to the livery to check on the horses. He found Axel busy mucking out the stalls.

'Were you surprised this morning to find three extra horses?'

'Kind of,' said Axel. 'I could tell from the brands they were from the YJ.'

At that moment Ludie Lundstrom came in with only a frown for a greeting.

'Good morning, Mr Lundstrom.'

'Not so very good. A terrible thing when people die the way they did this morning.'

'Dying's a terrible thing no matter how it happens,' said Royce.

'Worse, I think, when you make it happen.'

Axel looked at his father as if he'd said something wrong, then looked quickly to see what Royce would say.

'We'll be staying in town a while. Will you take care of our horses?'

'That's what I do. I take care of horses.'

'Thank you, Mr Lundstrom.'

Then Royce left, feeling once again

the unpleasant weight of a good man's disapproval.

During the day there was a fair amount of cautious activity on the part of the citizens of Jawbone. People came together in clusters, then separated to continue their discussions in other clusters. Late that afternoon a small contingent of them came into The Last Apache to call on Jamerson.

A stern faced Zachary Phelps from the bank was leading, with Arthur Winston and two other men close behind and Doc Haney trailing with a bemused expression of not really wanting to be a part of it all. As they entered the saloon, they looked from Miles behind the bar to Royce sitting at a table.

'We want to see Jamerson,' said Phelps.

'What about?' said Royce.

'About what it'll take to make him leave this town alone.'

'And let it grow,' added Winston.

'I could be wrong,' said Royce, 'but I

don't think there's anything you can say that will get him to do that. We'll see.'

He went upstairs to Jamerson's room and found Malone sitting in a chair pulled up next to the bed. He and Jamerson were playing cards.

'What's up?' said Malone.

'A peace party. They want to talk.'

'Sure,' said Jamerson. 'Now that Foley's dead, they're back to talking. But fine, let them come up. Just two or three. At least they'll be more interesting than this card game.'

Malone grinned at Royce. 'I've been winning.'

Royce brought up Phelps, Winston, and Haney. They squeezed into the small room and stood looking down at Jamerson as he lay propped up in bed.

'You back so soon, Doc?' said Jamerson.

'It's not a professional visit,' he said drily, then deferred to Phelps.

'Mr Jamerson,' said Phelps, 'we have a problem.'

'Then you're lucky. I have more than

one, starting with this shot-up leg.'

'I hope you're not injured too badly,' said Phelps, not very convincingly.

'What you really mean is you wish I'd been injured a whole lot worse, to the point I wouldn't have needed Doc's services.'

'I don't want to get personal about this.'

'I do! Getting shot is always personal, and you're the one who brought Foley here to do it.'

'It was the town's decision to bring in — '

'Bring in a legalized gunman to take care of me.'

'No, to establish some real law here in Jawbone. In spite of what you think, Mr Jamerson, you are not the law, and the rest of us have a right to live and work and prosper. We've come to ask you to reconsider your position.'

'That's right, Mr Jamerson,' said Winston. 'Why can't you be a part of this community instead of standing against it all the time?'

'If I had wanted to be part of a community, I would've stayed back East. This land was meant to be wild and free.'

Phelps said, 'You're the one who fenced in the land with all your wire.'

'Which I bought at no small price from Winston here. You should take your goods and your gains and move on to some other 'community' and leave me and the land the way we were before you came.'

'Look here,' said Winston, 'you can't expect us just to pack up and leave.'

'I don't expect anything,' said Jamerson. 'I take the actions that need taking. What you do then is up to you.'

'Your actions included cutting off our water,' said Phelps. 'You must've expected consequences when you did that.'

'I haven't cut off your water entirely,' said Jamerson, pulling himself up a little higher in bed. 'But that's a pretty good idea, and I think I'll do it.'

Phelps colored quickly in anger. 'You

would do that, wouldn't you!' He took a step forward. 'Someone ought to — '

Malone made a movement toward Phelps, who stopped abruptly.

'Someone ought to what?' said Jamerson. 'Go out and hire a faster gun than Foley? Obviously you're not going to do anything yourself.'

'Oh, what's the use?' said Phelps, turning away to the door.

Winston said to Haney, 'Let's go,' and followed Phelps out of the room.

Haney paused at the doorway and looked squarely at Royce. It was a wondering kind of look, full of incomprehension, unspoken, yet clear in its implied rebuke.

Jamerson said, 'You have something to say, Doc?'

Haney looked his way. 'Yes. Next time you need me, come to my office.' Then he walked out.

Jamerson chuckled. 'I like Haney. That attitude of his comes from having the power of life and death in his hands.'

Royce shook his head. 'I doubt if he'd claim the power over either one.'

That evening Royce brought Jamerson his supper from Betsy's Café. Betsy didn't ask any questions or offer any comments. She was all business as she packed the food in a hamper. The other patrons stopped talking while he was in the room and turned their attention to their plates.

Darkness was falling on the town when he got back to The Last Apache. He went up to Jamerson's room and began to unpack the still hot meal. Malone moved restlessly toward the door.

'Now that Royce is back, I think I'll go down and have a drink, maybe get in a card game, if it's all right.'

'Go ahead,' said Jamerson. 'I don't need both of you. I probably don't need either one of you, but you can never tell when some fool might decide to be a hero and take a shot at me.'

After Malone left, Jamerson sat up in bed and began to eat. Royce stood looking out the window.

'You've been moody all day,' said Jamerson. 'Something gnawing at you?'

'Doc asked me this morning if I could chloroform my conscience.'

'Having a conscience is fine, Royce, as long as you don't have it over the wrong things. The world's better off without Foley, Hawthorne, and Pratt.'

'Don't you suppose this town would say the same thing about you, me, and Malone?'

'I imagine they would. That's why a conscience isn't worth much. It's only a point of view and doesn't tell you anything.'

'Or maybe it does, and we don't know how to listen.'

Later in the evening, when the streets were empty and Malone was still downstairs playing cards, a quiet footstep sounded outside the door, followed by a soft knock. Instantly Royce was on his feet, gun drawn. Jamerson signaled for him to get in the corner behind the door.

'Come in,' said Jamerson.

The door opened. Royce couldn't see who walked in, but he could tell from the look on Jamerson's face there was no danger.

'I didn't expect to see you again this soon,' said Jamerson. 'Or at all, for that matter. Close the door.'

The door swung the other way, and there stood Darlene. She jumped a bit when she found Royce behind the door. He holstered his gun and regarded her with what he hoped was no expression, because he didn't want to show what he was feeling right then.

'Should I leave?' he asked.

'No,' said Jamerson. 'I might need your protection, depending on what our visitor came to do.'

'I wouldn't think you'd need protecting from that,' said Royce.

Darlene gave him a look that was both angry and dismayed, then turned to Jamerson.

'I was hoping I'd find you alone.'

Royce said, 'You came up the back

way? Like always?'

She whirled around. 'There is no 'always.' No matter what you're thinking, you're wrong.'

Jamerson suddenly laughed. 'That's funny, all right.'

Darlene stepped closer to the bed. 'I heard you were shot. Believe it or not, I came to see how you were.'

'That's even funnier. But I'm expected to recover. Sorry to disappoint you.'

'You disappointed me a long time ago. That doesn't mean I want you to die.'

'I'm almost touched. In fact, I definitely would be if I didn't know how much you hated me.'

'No, I don't hate you. I resent you and feel an abiding contempt for you, but the only time I came close to hating you was the night you let Blake try to kill Danny. And he would have if' — she half glanced over her shoulder — 'if Royce hadn't killed Blake instead. As soon as Danny told me what happened, I came up here to confront you, but you weren't in your room. Someone else was.' This time she looked directly at Royce. 'I didn't know then you were the one who saved Danny's life.'

Royce's mind was busy trying to rethink all his previous assumptions about Darlene and Jamerson.

'So you came to face Jamerson that night because Dan's your brother.'

'Because of that,' she said, 'and because Jamerson's my father.'

Royce stopped breathing for a moment. He looked at Jamerson for his reaction and saw him give a slow, calm nod of acknowledgment.

'I don't understand,' said Royce.

'In the early days of this town, before it could hardly be called a town, my mother was a single woman who was foolish enough to get involved with a married man. A man who refused to stand by her when she got pregnant.'

'Don't try to say I abandoned her,' said Jamerson, 'because I didn't. I supported her as long as she needed it.'

'In secret. It's all been a secret, hasn't it? From everyone. All these years.'

'Your mother found someone else.'

'A good man. A much better man than you.'

Royce said, 'Arthur Winston.'

'He moved to town much later. They got married when I was little, but I wasn't too little to know who my real father was, and Yale knew that I knew. Mother made me promise never to tell anyone. Then she had Danny. She died giving him life.' She faced Jamerson again with a sudden anger. 'And you were going to take that life. Don't tell me you weren't, even though it was Blake doing it.'

'I never told Blake to go after Dan.'

'But you didn't stop him, either. Danny's life didn't matter to you. Or maybe it did. Maybe he was too much of a reminder of my mother. You couldn't get rid of her daughter, but you could gun down her son, or at least try.'

'Ridiculous. Dan doesn't mean anything to me one way or the other.'

'That might be the saddest truth of all, if I could believe you had any truth in you.'

'If I wanted Dan dead, he'd be dead. Would I have been sorry if Blake killed him? Not really. How's that for truth? And here's some more. You wouldn't have been sorry if Foley had killed *me*. Would you?'

Darlene was quiet for a moment, regaining control. 'The sad fact of the matter is . . . I would have been sorry. Just sorry for all the things that never were.'

She walked out of the room then, turning to leave by the back stairs. Royce shut the door again, and Jamerson sighed.

'Darlene's mother was a beautiful woman, just like Darlene. But I didn't love her. I loved my wife. Yes, I know what you're thinking. If I loved her, how could I betray her with another woman? It was the weakness of a young man. Nothing more. Then Darlene was born. I couldn't take her away from her mother, and frankly I didn't want to. Perhaps if she had been a boy . . . '

'A son,' said Royce, catching the implication.

'Yes. I might've taken him in, and maybe Sarah would've understood, but what would I have done with the boy's mother? No, it was just impossible. Luckily, Arthur Winston's arrival in town solved the problem. Darlene got a new father.'

'And later a brother.'

'Half-brother. And no kin of mine.'

Royce didn't know whether to pity this man or despise him. He found himself doing both.

Malone came up after another hour. He was in a good mood because he had come out ahead in his card game, though all he had won was a dollar.

'I was down by sixteen at one point,' he said. 'I was never so happy to see three jacks in that last hand. Anything happen up here?'

Jamerson looked at Royce, who said, 'All quiet.'

16

The next day they returned to the ranch, and Jamerson's first order was to close the dam entirely, shutting off the last flow of water. He sent Royce and Malone out to do it the way he had showed them weeks before.

'This should get the town's attention,' said Malone as they neared the dam.

'It isn't right, you know,' said Royce.

'Right? That's kind of beside the point, isn't it?'

'It shouldn't be.'

'You backing out?' said Malone.

'I told Jamerson I'd do what he wanted as long as I was working for him. So that's what I'm going to do today. What I do tomorrow may be something different.'

They dismounted and climbed the logs at the end of the dam to reach the top. The water was backed up far to the north, spreading in a vast lake that filled every gully, gulch, and arroyo. On the south side of the dam a narrow rush of water flowed through the opening, creating a modest stream in the much wider riverbed.

Malone reached over and with both hands pulled the lever to release the heavy door, sending it falling into place. The southern gush of water abruptly stopped, with barely a trickle escaping around the edges of the door.

'Done,' said Malone. 'And no one tried to stop us.'

'No one knew about it.'

'They will now.'

'A river ought to be able to flow wherever it goes. And people ought to be able to use it the way they want.'

'This one flows to right here,' said Malone, smiling. 'And Yale's using it the way he wants.'

Royce shook his head. 'You have a way of twisting things around to make them sound OK, even when they're not.'

As Malone headed back to report to

Jamerson, Royce rode toward town along the riverbank, watching the water pool in small depressions. He recalled what the river looked like when he first crossed it, with the water up to his horse's knees. Even then it had looked low. Now it looked barren, just a series of mud puddles.

As he drew closer to Jawbone, he saw people standing along the edge of the river, staring at its emptiness. He reined in, then circled around a different way into town.

Royce wanted to see just one person today, though he doubted she wanted to see him. He wasted no time in riding to her shop and going inside. As he imagined, she offered no smile to greet his entrance.

'If you have any questions about anything,' said Darlene, 'I'm not answering them.'

He knew she was referring to Jamerson. 'I'm not asking any questions. I'm here to apologize.'

Her face lost some of its displeasure.

'Apologize for what?'

'For certain conclusions I jumped to. I was relieved to find out I was wrong.'

'You've been wrong about a lot of things, Royce. And as long as you keep working for Jamerson, you'll continue to be wrong. There's only so much you can apologize for.'

He nodded, not wanting to admit out loud that she was right. He tried to change the subject.

'So, have you ordered those hymnals yet?'

'Not much point in that,' she said, casting a rueful glance out the window. 'I doubt if Jawbone will ever have a church . . . or anyone left to go to it.'

'Not with the river all dried up.' As soon as he said it, her expression told him that she hadn't heard yet. 'Today Jamerson shut the dam completely.'

'And you let him.'

'As you said, as long as I work for him, I have a lot to apologize for.'

'And as long as you work for him, there can't be anything — ' Her eyes fell away as she wavered.

'Anything between you and me,' he finished for her.

'It sounds presumptuous for me to say it. But it's how I feel.'

Royce reached out and took her hand. 'Saying it tells me how you feel about a lot of things.' And then he let her hand go.

There wasn't much else to say between them. He rode back through town, stopping when he came abreast of the empty jail. It reminded him of other jails he had seen, years after they were abandoned, when their timbers were rotting, grayed by the sun, and their bars had rusted. He had seen whole towns that way, deserted, unable to survive.

Royce spurred his horse and rode on back to the YJ.

For several days Jamerson stayed in a dismal frame of mind, despite his victory over Foley. His leg healed fast enough, allowing him to walk without difficulty, and yet he grew more and more disquieted, as though whatever was troubling him wouldn't let him rest. Then one morning he called Royce and Malone into his study.

'Any news from Jawbone?'

'Only talk,' said Royce.

'Nobody's moving out now that the river's dry?'

'Maybe a few,' said Malone. 'But remember they've still got some wells.'

Jamerson scowled. 'They could hold out a long time with wells.'

'Unless something happened to the wells,' said Malone.

Royce spoke up. 'Poisoning wells may not be a hanging offense, but it ought to be.'

'Nobody's poisoning anything,' said Jamerson. 'But I'm tired of Jawbone. Tired of its people and tired of its memories . . . and just plain tired of fighting against it.'

'You're giving in to the town?' said Malone.

Jamerson clenched his jaw as a cold, black anger came into his eyes. 'No, I'm not giving in to it. I'm going to burn it.'

'Burn it!' said Royce. 'You can't burn out a whole town.'

'Shakespeare said, 'Suit the action to the word, the word to the action'.' If I give the word, the action will follow. I've got enough men to do it.'

'But will they do it?' asked Royce.

'Will you?'

Royce didn't have to think before he answered. 'No, I won't. Fighting Foley was one thing, but burning the homes and businesses of innocent people is going too far.'

Jamerson turned to Malone. 'Is it too far for you?'

Malone shrugged. 'They won't put up much fight. We'll ride in, and we'll ride the people out. Nobody'll get burned up, Royce. Rabbits run before a fire.'

Royce ignored Malone and fixed his eyes on Jamerson. 'I said I'd do what you told me to as long as I worked for you. As of right now, I don't work for you anymore.'

'Fine,' said Jamerson. 'What we're

going to do doesn't need any fancy gunplay. Leave if you want.'

Royce said nothing more. He headed to the bunkhouse to get his gear and was packing his saddle-bags when Malone came in.

'You're being a fool, you know,' said Malone. 'You're leaving when all the fighting's done and we've won.'

'I don't believe the people in Jawbone are going to let Jamerson burn their town without a fight, and that means killing people who don't deserve being killed.'

'I've got a hunch this has something to do with Darlene Mueller.'

'It's got nothing to do with her,' said Royce, though it sounded hollow when he said it. 'I'm not a marauder, riding with a gang and burning towns. I've never done that, and I won't start now.' He cinched up his saddle-bags and slung them over his shoulder.

'So where are you heading now? Just to some other job, same as you've been doing here.'

'Maybe not this time.'

'Oh, sure. You're gonna go homestead a little farm and plant some peas and corn.'

'I like peas and corn.'

'You might like eating them, but you won't like growing them.'

Royce walked out of the bunkhouse to his horse with Malone following.

'If you ride out, you better ride on,' said Malone. 'What I mean is, don't do anything stupid, like get in Jamerson's way.'

'Because then I'd be in your way.'

'And we wouldn't want that.'

Royce swung up into the saddle. 'So long, Malone. Think about what I said.'

'And you think about what I said.'

'Looks like we've both got our share of thinking to do.'

Then Royce gave a nod of farewell and rode off, leaving Malone looking after him.

17

By the time Royce got to Jawbone, he knew what he was going to do and how he was going to do it. He just didn't know what would follow from it.

First he stopped at the bank and withdrew the bonus money Jamerson had paid him. Next he went to the General Mercantile, where Arthur Winston gave him a hard stare when he entered.

'I'm here to buy something,' said Royce. 'Something I saw in your storeroom.'

Not stopping, he continued straight to the back with Winston right behind him. He found Dan working there, opening boxes. Quickly Royce looked around for the particular crate he had seen before.

'What are you looking for?' asked Dan.

'This.' Royce stopped in front of the

crate of dynamite that Foley had ordered, but never got a chance to use.

'Dynamite?' said Winston. 'You want to buy dynamite? What for?'

'I want to blow something up. No, not the town,' he said, answering Winston's suspicious look. 'And I'm not going to flood it, either. Jawbone's far enough from the river and high enough that it won't be hit by the water when it comes.'

'You're going to blow up the dam!' said Dan.

'I don't understand,' said Winston. 'Why does Jamerson want to blow up his own dam?'

'He doesn't,' said Royce. 'I'm doing this on my own.'

'You quit him?'

'I reckon if I hadn't quit already, this would sure enough get me fired.'

He reached for a crowbar and pried open the lid of the crate, revealing sticks of dynamite packed in sawdust.

'Do either of you know how to use this stuff?'

'What's to know?' said Dan. 'You wrap 'em together, stick 'em where you want 'em to go, then light the fuse and run.'

'I don't think it's that simple,' said his father.

'Simple enough,' said Royce. 'But I'll need some help doing it, and we need to do it right now.'

'In daylight?' said Winston. 'Wouldn't it be better to wait till night?'

'Can't take the chance of waiting. Jamerson's talking about burning the town.'

'The whole town?' said Dan.

Winston said, 'How will blowing the dam stop him?'

'I don't know if it'll stop him,' said Royce, 'but it'll give him something else to think about.'

'He'll be gunning for you then.'

'I suppose he will. But I don't gun so easy.'

'I'll help you set the dynamite,' said Dan.

'No, you won't,' said Winston. 'If it's

necessary, I'll go.'

Royce considered how the shop-keeper had to limp his way around and said, 'That knee of yours works all right on level ground, but not where we'll have to go. Dan would be a big help.'

Winston looked at his son's eager face, then back at Royce. 'You saved his life before. I'm counting on you to keep him safe this time, too.'

'I will,' said Royce. 'We'll put the dynamite in saddle-bags, then ride through the south gate to get to the dam.'

'They won't stop you?' said Winston.

'They may try,' said Royce, but the way he said it made it clear that he didn't plan on letting anyone stop him. Then he pulled the bank envelope from his pocket and handed it to Winston. 'Here. Take the cost of the dynamite out of this. I'll come back for what's left.' At least he hoped he would.

A short time later Royce and Dan rode to the YJ. Royce had refused to let Dan bring a gun. And now as they approached the south gate, he reminded Dan to let him do the talking. As expected, two guards came out of the shack to meet them.

'Hey, Royce,' said one. 'We heard you quit.'

'You heard right. Time for me to ride on. Going north.'

The other guard pointed to Dan and said, 'What about him?'

'He's going, too. Not much future for a young man in Jawbone.'

The guard laughed. 'Not much future in Jawbone for anyone.'

Royce pulled out some money. 'Since I don't work for the YJ anymore, here's the toll for me and my friend.'

'First toll we've collected all week!' said the guard.

'Be seeing you, Royce,' said the other one, opening the gate.

Then Royce and Dan rode on through, moving casually as if they were in no particular hurry.

'That was easy,' said Dan in a low voice.

'Easier than it'll be riding back.'

It wasn't long before they spotted the ranch house off to the west, half a mile from the road. Royce also saw a small group of men gathered at one of the corrals. That was unusual for this time of day, but he could guess the reason for it. Then something happened that made his heartbeat quicken. The whole group of men turned and looked his way. He knew at this distance they couldn't see him clearly, but still they might recognize him and the way he sat his horse. If so, Jamerson would surely wonder what he was doing here and where he was going.

'We may not have much time,' said Royce.

As soon as they were out of view, they spurred their horses on. Eventually they left the road and angled off to the dried-up riverbed. When Dan caught his first sight of the dam, he couldn't believe how big it was.

'If I had known it was this grand, I

would've paid the toll just to come and see it!'

'Wait'll you see the water stacked up behind it,' said Royce.

At the base of the dam they dismounted and began setting the bundled sticks of dynamite into crevices in the close-fitted timbers.

'You think this will blow all the way through?' said Dan.

'If it doesn't, the weight of the water should do the rest.'

They fastened four fuses from the dynamite to one longer fuse and stretched it out. They were just about to light it when they heard riders coming.

'Dan, grab our horses and take them up the bluff.' He pointed to the east side of the riverbank, away from the riders. 'Wait till I signal you, then come back down and light the fuse.'

'What are you going to do?'

'I'm wondering that myself. Go on now.'

As Dan led the horses over the bluff, Royce scrambled up the other side and quickly climbed on to the dam. He saw now there were three riders coming: one of them was Malone.

Reaching the very top of the dam, Royce called out to the riders as they came to a stop.

'Hello, boys.'

Malone said, 'What are you doing up there, Royce?'

'Enjoying the view.'

Malone grinned. 'What else?'

'Just passing the time of day, now that I'm out of a job. Why are you so curious?'

'Not me. It's Jamerson. He's the one who wants to know.'

'Then tell him to come and ask me himself.'

'Why don't you ride back with us?'

'I'm not inclined to do that, Malone.'

Malone scanned the area. Royce hoped he wouldn't spot the fuse lying on the ground.

'What happened to your friend?' said Malone.

'Which one?'

'It's good to have so many friends you can't keep track of them. But I meant the one who's hiding with the horses over yonder.'

'He's shy. Gun shy.'

'Nobody's doing any shooting. Yet.'

'Ride on back, Malone.'

'Can't do that, Royce. Not unless you come with me.'

'I'm not going with you.'

Malone sat very still in his saddle, obviously thinking over his options, what he did or didn't want to do. Finally he turned to the other two men, Hank and Jordan.

'Go get him and bring him down.'

They looked at each other with unspoken reservations about that chore, but then dismounted and headed up the west end of the dam. Royce stood calmly above them, waiting.

'Now, don't give us any trouble, Royce,' said Hank, the one in the lead as he got near the top.

'Wouldn't think of it,' said Royce, just before he kicked him in the head, sending him bouncing backward down the uneven endings of the logs. Hank groaned as he hit the bottom, grabbing a broken arm.

Jordan had dodged to avoid a collision, but now he scurried up the final few steps and rushed at Royce with wild swings that forced him back. Royce countered with fast, accurate punches and knocked him down. Lying on his side, Jordan swung his boot around to catch Royce on his upper calf, raking him with the rowel of his spur. Royce winced with the pain and jumped away.

Jordan scrambled to his feet and came at him with renewed effort. Several quick exchanges of blows put Jordan on his back again. In anger and frustration, sitting halfway up, he went for his gun. Royce drew and fired. Jordan fell over, but struggled to rise, blood oozing from his side, his gun still in his hand.

'Drop it or die,' said Royce, ready to shoot again if he had to, but not wanting to.

Jordan dropped his gun. Then Royce helped him up and walked him to the end of the dam.

'Go join Hank. Ride on back and tell Jamerson he better open an account with Doc Haney.'

Grunting and swearing, Jordan, with difficulty, made his way down off the dam.

Malone smiled and shook his head. As Hank and Jordan struggled on to their horses, he slowly dismounted and headed calmly toward the dam. Royce waited till Malone had started climbing up and the others were riding off before he called out to Dan.

'Do what you need to do, Dan, and ride away. I'll catch up to you later.'

'I wouldn't count on that,' said Malone from below, taking his time.

Royce backed up along the top of the dam to put some distance between himself and Malone. He watched as Dan ran down the riverbank, struck a match, lit the fuse, then ran back up to his horse, all unseen by Malone, who was carefully choosing his steps as he climbed. Dan was already riding away when Malone finally appeared, still smiling as he gained the top of the dam. He advanced until he was twenty feet from Royce, then stopped.

Royce waited, facing Malone while being mindful of the burning fuse down below. He couldn't see any good way this was going to end.

'Well,' said Malone. 'Here we are.'

'Looks like it.'

'What do we do now?'

'That's up to you, at least for the next sixty seconds or so.'

'What happens after sixty seconds?'

Royce nodded down to his left and Malone looked over the edge. The fuse was sparking and smoking as it moved toward the dam.

'So that's what you're up to,' said Malone.

'I suggest you hurry that way to your horse and I'll head this way to mine, and we can both get off this dam alive.'

'You know it can't be that way,

Royce. I'd just have to come after you later on.'

'You want this gunfight, don't you?'

'Funny thing about that. I want the gunfight, but I don't want to kill you.'

'I don't want you to kill me, either.'

Malone grinned. Then a loud hiss from below made both men look. The main fuse had reached its connection to the other four, igniting them and sending them burning toward their caches of dynamite.

'If you're gonna draw on me, Malone, you better do it quick.'

'It wouldn't be very sporting if I drew first.'

'I'm not drawing on you.'

'Afraid you can't beat me?'

'Maybe I'm afraid I can.'

'The chance of dying doesn't bother me,' said Malone. 'That's just part of the game, isn't it?'

'It's not a game to me.'

'Which is why you'll likely be the one to die.'

'If you wait any longer, we'll both

die. Now draw if that's what you're set to do.'

'I've got an idea. Remember how we drew on Drake and Kyle when we heard the crow?'

'I don't hear any crows, Malone.'

'We'll both draw when the dam explodes.'

'That's crazy!' said Royce. 'I never counted on getting shot and blown up at the same time.'

Malone laughed. 'Or you can draw on me now and maybe still get away.'

'We could both get away if you'd call this off.'

'Seconds to go. Have you ever wondered what dying is like? I've seen many men die, but I still don't have any idea.'

'You seem in an awful hurry to find out.'

'In a way I'm sorry it had to be you, Royce. In another way I'm glad.'

Royce could hear the fuses spitting twenty feet below. 'Malone — '

'Whether I kill you, or you kill me,

you're somebody I respect.'

Then Malone stopped talking and set himself, hand by his gun, smile on his face. Royce's body tensed, waiting for the explosion. Any second now. One second, two, three . . .

The blast blew out the bottom half of the dam with a deafening roar, and both men drew and fired as the dam collapsed beneath them, knocking them off their feet and jolting their aim. Royce felt a bullet rip through him just above the right side of his collarbone and at the same time saw Malone spin from the impact of his shot, though he couldn't tell where it hit him. There was no second shot from either man as they fell with the upper portion of the dam into a torrent of water that carried them away in a rampaging flood down the river course.

The wall of water swept along at great speed, overflowing the banks on either side. Royce struggled to keep his head above the surface and avoid getting struck by the broken logs of the dam, now dangerous battering rams that raced and swirled all around him. He reached out and managed to throw an arm over one of the logs, then hung on tightly for the tumultuous ride. Only then did he have a chance to look around for Malone, but couldn't see him anywhere.

Off to his left he spotted Dan sitting astride his horse and watching from a rise, his eyes wide open at the spectacle passing by. Royce couldn't tell if Dan saw him or not. Then Dan was behind him, and the water rushed on.

Finally the water evened out a bit, but remained too treacherous to swim in. Royce sped past the ranch house, which he could barely make out in the distance to his right. He had already traveled miles in much less time than he could've ridden the same distance, and he began to wonder if he might have to ride this river clean out of the territory.

The logs were scattering by now, many of them washing off to one side or the other, so Royce began to kick with his legs, trying to guide the direction of the log he clung to. Long, arduous minutes passed as he slowly managed to edge closer and closer to the right riverbank. Holding onto the log, kicking with all his might, he had nearly exhausted himself by the time he gained the shallows at one of the widest parts of the riverbed. Turning loose of the log, he swam a short way farther and found his feet for a moment before the current knocked him over and sent him swimming again. One more try and he clawed his way on to land. He lay there panting, glad to be alive, and only then did he feel the pain at the side of his neck and remember he'd been shot. He raised his head to see where he was: there stood Jawbone, no more than a quarter mile away.

Rising unsteadily to his feet, he looked behind him at the swift-running river as the water kept pouring out through the broken dam far upstream. He wondered about Malone and about Dan and about his horse on the other side of the river. Then he realized he'd dropped his Colt when the dam fell. So there he stood, drenched and shot; no gun, no horse, no hat. And he laughed.

'What a ride!' he said out loud.

Then he noticed his shirt was turning pink, so he clapped a hand over his wound and started walking toward town. A crowd of people had gathered at the riverbank, and several of them saw him coming and ran to meet him. For a moment he wished he had his gun. Then he saw their smiles. Arthur Winston was among them.

'Royce!' he cried, running up. 'You did it!' He looked beyond him with concern. 'Where's Dan?'

'He's all right. Stranded on the other side, no doubt.'

'I told the folks what you were going to do.'

Several voices spoke up, thanking and congratulating him. He wasn't used to that and hardly knew how to respond.

'You're bleeding,' said Winston.

'Yeah, that's getting to be a habit. Is

Doc Haney here?'

'Yes, yes,' came a weary voice from behind him as Haney walked up. 'Where have you been shot this time?'

'It's not too bad. The bullet went through.'

'Come on, then. Let's go take care of it.'

Royce followed him back to his house, though his legs were wobbly from all he'd been through. He was grateful to sit still and rest while Haney cleaned out the wound and bandaged it.

'I'm just curious,' said Haney. 'Did you get shot this often before you came to Jawbone?'

'No, as a matter of fact, I didn't.'

'Do you like getting shot?'

'Not especially.'

'You might want to put those two answers together and figure out what you should do next.'

'If you're suggesting I leave town, I can't do that just yet.'

'Some particular reason?'

'Several,' said Royce.

Haney didn't ask what they were. Royce pulled his wet, ripped, blood-stained shirt back on and headed straight for the General Mercantile, where he found Winston back in his store.

'Do I have enough money left over from the dynamite to pay for a new outfit? I need a change of clothes, a hat, and a six-gun.'

'Take whatever you need,' said Winston.

Royce quickly went around the store, picking up the items he required, then stepped into the back to change. When he came out, Winston handed him the bank envelope with money still inside.

'You sure I've got this much left?' said Royce.

'Foley had paid a deposit on the dynamite. So what are you going to do now?'

'There's somebody I need to find.'

'Darlene?'

Royce smiled at his suggestion. 'That

would be a lot more pleasant, but no. If you see her, well, I guess by now she knows I'm no longer working for Jamerson.'

'Jamerson knows it, too, so watch yourself.'

Next Royce went to the livery stable, where Mr Lundstrom and Axel met him with great smiles of welcome. He asked Lundstrom how much it would cost to borrow a horse and saddle for a day.

'Borrow? Nothing. No charge for borrowing. Not today. Not for you.'

'Thanks,' said Royce.

'No, we thank you. We have water again!'

Axel brought the horse around and threw a saddle on him. In his excitement he said, 'Are you going to kill Mr Jamerson?'

'Axel,' said his father sternly, 'that's not a question to ask.' Then he, too, looked at Royce for the answer.

'I don't plan on killing anybody, Axel. Unless they force me to.'

And then he was on his way, riding north again to look for Malone.

18

Royce rode close beside the river, which had settled down now and was flowing strong and wide. And as he rode, it wasn't just Malone he was looking for — he kept scanning the far side of the river for any sight of Dan.

All along the way there were splintered logs from the great dam, lying where they'd been left by the flood or bobbing fitfully in the shallows. Royce knew Malone had plunged into the water when the dam blew up. If he hadn't been injured too badly, he might have been able to swim to shore. If not, his body might be miles and miles downstream by now, still riding the current.

Suddenly he heard a voice call out to him from across the river. He looked over and there was Dan, riding one horse and leading another.

'I went back for your horse!' yelled Dan.

'Have you seen anyone?' shouted Royce. 'Any sign of Malone?'

'No. How are you? I saw you in the river.'

'I'm fine. You may have to ride several more miles downstream before you can cross.'

'Where are you going?'

'To settle things. I'll see you back in Jawbone.'

Dan nodded and rode on south, while Royce kept going north. Soon he came to where the barbed wire fence met the river on both sides, and on both sides several yards of it were down, torn away by the powerful rush of water before it receded. Royce understood now how Dan had gotten around the fence. He looked off to his left toward the south gate in the distance. So far as he could tell, nobody was standing guard, though it was possible they were in the shack. He decided to find out, since he didn't want to face them later in circumstances he couldn't yet guess.

He rode up inside the fence line till he got close, then dismounted and quietly approached the shack. Still no sign of anyone and no horses. He was pretty sure it was deserted. He drew his gun, then edged up to the door and found it standing open. Inside on the floor lay Malone.

'Malone!'

Royce holstered his gun and knelt beside him, slowly turning him over. Malone grunted. At least he was alive, though he was soaked and bloody. There was a single bullet wound between his ribs where Royce's shot had landed. Malone opened his eyes.

'So you made it, too,' he said, sounding surprised to see Royce.

'Can you sit up?'

'With a little help.'

Royce lifted him enough to get him into a chair, where Malone grimaced from the pain.

'We need to get you to Doc Haney.'

Malone's grimace turned to half a grin. 'Yeah. Good idea.' Then he ran his eyes up and down Royce's body. 'You mean I missed you?'

'No, you got me here.' He pointed to where the bandage raised a bulge under his shirt.

'Shows you how an exploding dam can throw off your aim. Well, my aim anyway.'

'The place you were standing fell away faster than mine did.'

'Sounds like a good enough excuse to me,' said Malone.

'I rode the river all the way to Jawbone and got fixed up.'

'Smart. I crawled out at the fence line and made my way up here. The place was empty. Then I remembered. Yale was calling all the men in for his barbecue, the one he had planned for Jawbone.'

'I wonder what he'll do now.'

'To tell you the truth, Royce, that's not real high on my list of concerns right now.' Then he laughed briefly, catching himself, clutching his wound.

'Did the bullet go through?'

'It found itself a nice little home. A little souvenir from one of the fastest guns I ever faced. But on solid ground I would've beat you, Royce.'

'I know.'

Malone glanced down at his boots, which were caked with mud.

'My poor boots. They look nearly as bad as I feel.'

Royce couldn't do anything about Malone's wound, but at least he could do something about his boots. He knelt down and wiped away the mud with a handkerchief until the leather was showing.

'Thanks for that,' said Malone, seemingly moved by the gesture. Then with a smile he added, 'I don't suppose you have any polish on you?'

Suddenly Royce heard horses coming, and more than a few.

'Riders,' he said.

He stepped to the door and looked up the road. Jamerson and about a dozen cowhands were riding this way.

'Jamerson?' said Malone.

'Yeah.'

'Doesn't look like he's gonna let a little water stop him from burning the town. And you and that one gun of yours aren't going to stop him, either. I'd loan you mine, but I lost it in the river when I was too busy holding my guts together.'

The riders were much closer now. The hoofbeats of their galloping horses grew in volume, bringing the inescapable. There was nothing Royce could do.

Malone's voice broke into his thoughts. 'Hand me that canteen, will you?'

'Fine time for a drink,' said Royce, reaching for the canteen they kept in the shack.

'Yeah, you'd think I would've had enough water for today, wouldn't you?'

Royce handed it to him. 'You probably shouldn't drink too much.'

'Afraid I'll leak?'

The riders were almost to the shack

as Royce turned away from Malone. Quickly Malone reached out and snatched Royce's gun from its holster.

'Hey!' said Royce, spinning around.

'Sorry, but I just don't feel right without a gun.'

Royce looked at the barrel pointed directly at his middle. There was no way Malone could miss him at this distance, even in his current condition.

Malone struggled to his feet, his free hand pressed against his wound. He took a couple of unsteady steps forward, walking slightly hunched over.

'Go on,' he said. 'Outside.'

At gunpoint Royce stepped out of the shack, just as Jamerson and his hands rode up and stopped. Malone stood in the doorway, leaning against the frame for support.

Jamerson looked down at Royce with a cold regard.

'Good work, Malone. You got him.'

'We kind of got each other.'

'You double-crossed me, Royce.'

'I crossed you,' said Royce, 'but it

wasn't a double-cross.'

'You can't deny you turned against me. You blew up my dam and shot up my men. You should've just ridden out, Royce. That was your mistake. And I trusted you. That was mine. But it's one I won't make again. Malone, finish him.'

Malone straightened himself in the doorway, bracing for the task at hand. Royce said nothing. He had figured his life would end this way sooner or later.

'I've killed a lot of men through the years,' said Malone, 'but I never had the chance to do what I'm going to do now. You see . . . I've always wanted to kill me a really rich man.'

And with that he shot Jamerson out of the saddle. He landed dead with two bullets in his chest. The other men were too surprised to react. A couple of them halfway went for their guns, but thought better of it. Royce looked around at Malone in amazement and saw that wicked little smile on his face.

'You can gun me down if you want

to,' said Malone to the riders, 'but there's nobody going to pay you for it.' When no one contradicted that logic, he nodded toward Jamerson. 'Take him home, fellas. No use riding into Jawbone now.'

Several of the men dismounted and slung Jamerson's body across his horse, then the whole bunch headed slowly back up the road. As Royce watched them go, he heard a noise and turned to see Malone slump to the ground. He rushed to his side.

'Not dead yet,' muttered Malone.

'Glad to hear it . . . and thanks.'

'My pleasure.'

Royce raised him up so he could sit with his back leaning against the shack. He didn't know how much longer Malone could hold out, but he knew his only hope was Doc Haney.

'I'll get the doctor. Your best bet is to rest here and not move around. I'll be back as fast as I can.'

'I wager I'll still be here when you get back.' He gave Royce that same

271

mocking smile, as if nothing in the world mattered.

Royce picked up his gun, then ran to his horse and hurried off to Jawbone. Doc Haney grabbed his bag when he heard the news, and together they rode back to the south gate.

Royce had made the trip as fast as he could, but it still took him a couple of hours. As soon as the shack came into view, something else drew his attention. Overhead, three buzzards were circling in the sky. He rode closer, horrified by what he saw next. A lone buzzard stood on the ground, pecking at Malone's body. Instantly Royce drew and fired, sending up a small eruption of black feathers. Then he and Haney rushed to where Malone was lying against the side of the shack.

'We're too late,' said Haney, stating the obvious.

Looking down at Malone, Royce saw the smile was gone from his face.

'For men like Malone and me, it's always too late.'

Since there was nothing Haney could do for Malone, he rode on to the ranch to attend to the men who were injured during the fight at the dam. Royce stayed behind because he had work to do. He wasn't going to give the buzzards any more chances.

That night, after his sad duty of burying Malone, Royce stayed in Jamerson's room at The Last Apache. He hadn't eaten all day, but he wasn't hungry. His patched up wound was hurting him, but he didn't care. He lay on the bed looking at the shadows on the ceiling, cast there by the low flame of the lamp.

When a knock sounded on the door, he reached for his gun out of habit, then stopped himself. What did it matter? He got up and opened the door.

'Hello,' said Darlene.

She stood there in the doorway just as she had on his first night in town.

'Seems like we've been here before,' said Royce.

'Except this time I knew who I would

find. May I come in?'

He stepped back to let her enter, then closed the door.

'How'd you know where I was?'

'The whole town knows. You've made a name for yourself here. A better name than before.'

He shook his head. 'No. Same name. Same man.'

'Danny said to tell you he left your horse at the livery. It took him several hours to find a place where he could ford the river.'

'That's what you came to tell me?'

'And Doc Haney says the two cowhands you fought are going to be fine.'

'Thanks for the report.'

'How are *you* doing?'

'I'll be OK,' said Royce. 'I suppose you've heard by now. Your father is dead.'

'Yale Jamerson is dead. He was never my father.' Her face grew pensive for a moment, then softened. 'So many things have changed since the last time we spoke. You turned against Yale, and you blew up the dam . . . '

'Which reminds me. If you still want to build that church, there's a whole lot of timber to be had for free, all up and down the river.'

'The point I was making is . . . you didn't do those things for yourself, but for the town. That means something.'

'What anything means is nothing I can figure out.'

She stepped closer to him. 'Can't you?'

For a second they stood there, trying to find answers in the other's eyes. Then Royce reached out and pulled her to him, drawing her into a kiss that she welcomed with an eager embrace. Kiss followed kiss, and in her arms he found a comfort he had seldom known. It was something more than passion, though passion was quickly gaining command. If Darlene were any other woman . . .

He drew back, and she questioned him with a look.

'Come on,' he said with just enough

resolve. 'I'm walking you home.'

She didn't try to dissuade him, but he could read a wistfulness in her eyes.

They walked down the back stairs together to the street. The night air helped to clear his mind. As they walked along in silence, a sudden thought came to him.

'Even though he never acknowledged you, Jamerson really was your father . . . which means you have an inheritance coming to you.'

Darlene laughed shortly. 'There would be no way to prove it. No one knew, because that was the way he wanted it.'

'All your life he cheated you. First when he was living. And now when he's dead.'

'He's gone. That's gift enough.'

After taking Darlene home, Royce returned to his room at The Last Apache. In the bureau he discovered a number of Jamerson's personal items — several books, an old watch, various small items of no particular worth. He thought they should be turned over to Jamerson's widow, so the next morning he rode out to the YJ. There was no one posted at the south gate to collect a toll. Jamerson's days of tyranny were over.

Royce knocked on the door of the ranch house and waited. After what seemed like a long time, Mrs Jamerson opened the door. He had half expected to find her dressed in black, but she appeared as she always had, though her face looked tired and drawn.

'Royce . . . please come in.'

'I didn't want to disturb you, but I thought you might like to have these things of your husband's. They were in his room at The Last Apache.'

He offered her the small bundle, which she took and set aside.

'Thank you. But please, do sit and talk with me for a moment.'

Feeling awkward, he followed her into the parlor.

'I'm sorry about Mr Jamerson,' he said, though he didn't feel sorry at all, except for the sadness it caused his widow.

Sitting in the morning light that filtered through the window, she looked older than before. She kept her hands folded in her lap.

'We were married a long time. We went through so much together. He was always kind to me, but I realize he treated others much differently. In any case, a violent death is to be expected out here.'

'I can't argue with that,' said Royce.

'What will you do now?' she asked.

'Me? I'm not sure.'

'I thought perhaps you and Miss Mueller . . . ' She trailed off. 'Have you talked to her since my husband's death?'

'Last night.'

'Did she . . . have anything to say?'

'About Mr Jamerson?'

'Yes.'

Suddenly, looking at Mrs Jamerson's strained face, Royce realized that she knew.

'We talked about her father,' he said, being careful how he phrased it in case he was wrong.

'Her father,' repeated Mrs Jamerson, regarding him closely. And then her face relaxed. 'She told you who he was. I'm glad.'

'You've known all along?'

'Yale and I never spoke of it, but I knew.'

'You should tell Darlene.'

'Now that he's gone, I will. And you can tell the people of Jawbone I'll open the roads again. The YJ will go back to being just a ranch like any other.'

'They'll be relieved to hear it.'

'And you know, Royce, you're welcome to stay on.'

It was an open door, an offer he only had to accept. But he couldn't. Stopping him was a deep awareness of what he had become through the years. He thanked her, then left the house and rode off the YJ for the last time, riding south with one more thing to do.

When he entered the shop, Darlene turned and smiled. He almost started to tell her about Mrs Jamerson, but that wasn't what he came in for, and he knew Mrs Jamerson would take care of it herself. Right now there was something else he had to tell her — he had to say goodbye.

'I'm about to ride out,' he said.

'Ride out where?'

'I don't know. Maybe someplace where I don't have to shoot anybody, and nobody's trying to shoot me.'

'You mean you're leaving? But why? Why not stay in Jawbone?'

'It's a hard thing to put into words, Darlene, but there's something far gone from inside me. It's the thing that lets a man live a satisfied life in a settled place. And as much as I might've dreamed of finding a place like that, I know that reaching for something you can't get hold of is a fool's play.'

'Then what will you do with your life?'

'Stay on the move. The funny thing about traveling is that hope always rides along, because you never know what's up ahead. But once you get there, it never seems enough. I wish it did.'

Tears glistened in Darlene's eyes. He was sorry he had hurt her, but he would've hurt her more the longer he stayed.

'Take care of yourself, then,' she said, trying to smile and not succeeding. 'Maybe someday you'll find your way back.'

'Maybe I will,' he said.

But going back the way he came was something he had never done before, and as he rode out of Jawbone heading west, he doubted he would ever find his way back. He doubted he would ever find his way at all.

We do hope that you have enjoyed reading this large print book.

Did you know that all of our titles are available for purchase?

We publish a wide range of high quality large print books including:
Romances, Mysteries, Classics
General Fiction
Non Fiction and Westerns

Special interest titles available in large print are:
The Little Oxford Dictionary
Music Book, Song Book
Hymn Book, Service Book

Also available from us courtesy of Oxford University Press:
Young Readers' Dictionary
(large print edition)
Young Readers' Thesaurus
(large print edition)

For further information or a free brochure, please contact us at:
Ulverscroft Large Print Books Ltd.,
The Green, Bradgate Road, Anstey,
Leicester, LE7 7FU, England.
Tel: (00 44) **0116 236 4325**
Fax: (00 44) **0116 234 0205**